S0-ARJ-449

# ABSOLUTELY MAYBE

## ALSO BY LISA YEE

*Millicent Min, Girl Genius*

*Stanford Wong Flunks Big-Time*

*So Totally Emily Ebers*


## FOR YOUNGER READERS

*Bobby vs. Girls (Accidentally)*

# LISA YEE

# ABSOLUTELY
# MAYBE

SCHOLASTIC INC.
New York  Toronto  London  Auckland
Sydney  Mexico City  New Delhi  Hong Kong

If you purchased this book without a cover, you should be aware that this book is stolen property. It was reported as "unsold and destroyed" to the publisher, and neither the author nor the publisher has received any payment for this "stripped book."

No part of this publication may be reproduced, stored in a retrieval system, or transmitted in any form or by any means, electronic, mechanical, photocopying, recording, or otherwise, without written permission of the publisher. For information regarding permission, write to Scholastic Inc., Attention: Permissions Department, 557 Broadway, New York, NY 10012.

ISBN 978-0-439-83845-0

Text copyright © 2009 by Lisa Yee
All rights reserved. Published by Scholastic Inc. SCHOLASTIC, the LANTERN LOGO, and associated logos are trademarks and/or registered trademarks of Scholastic Inc.

Arthur A. Levine Books hardcover edition designed by Elizabeth B. Parisi, published by Arthur A. Levine Books, an imprint of Scholastic Inc., February 2009.

12 11 10 9 8 7 6 5 4 3 2 1          10 11 12 13 14 15/0

Printed in the U.S.A.                    40
First Scholastic paperback printing, May 2010

★ **FOR KAIT** ★

**The author wishes to express her gratitude to**

**Arthur Levine, Cheryl Klein, Jodi Reamer,**

**the wonderful people at Thurber House,**

**and of course, Scott, Benny and, yes, Maggie.**

# ABSOLUTELY MAYBE

## ONE

The day I turned six, we went to the Magic Kingdom to celebrate, just my mom and me. We wore matching yellow sundresses trimmed with lace and straw hats with blue silk ribbons. Everyone told us we looked lovely. On Cinderella's Carousel, my horse was the only one with a golden bow on his tail. We went on It's a Small World three times, because I loved it so much. And when Captain Hook frightened me, my mother held me tight and sent him on his way.

At dinner, the waitress brought a slice of chocolate cake with six candles, and Belle, from *Beauty and the Beast*, sang "Happy Birthday" to me. Even though we were exhausted, we stayed at the theme park until after dark to watch the fireworks. When Tinkerbell appeared, I shut my eyes tight and wished that every day could be like this.

That night as my mother tucked me into bed, she brushed the hair out of my face and kissed me gently on the forehead.

"I love you, Mommy," I said.

"I love you too," she whispered. "We'll always have each other, Maybelline."

## ☆ T W O ☆

"You're not going to wear *that* to school, are you?" my mother asks as she takes another drag on her Virginia Slims.

In this house there are two things you can count on:

    1) That Chessy will hog the bathroom, and

    2) She will say, "You're not going to wear *that* to school, are you?"

I don't answer her. We both know I'm not going to change. As usual, I have on baggy jeans, a men's black Beefy Hanes T-shirt (XL), Converse so old they're held together with electrical tape, and Upton Sinclair's Army jacket. (He was husband number five of Chessy's six.)

"Sit down, Maybelline. It's time we had a little talk."

I check the clock. I'm late for school again.

"I have big news."

I frown. I know what "big news" means.

"Jake asked me to marry him!"

"Chessy, you just divorced Carlos and you're getting married again already?"

She ignores me. "You're going to be part of the wedding, so I want you to clean up your act. You will come out of your cocoon and turn into a beautiful butterfly if it kills us both. You will learn and adhere to Chessy's Seven Select Rules for Young Ladies. You will let your hair turn back to its natural color and then, if necessary, we will dye it blonde. And you will stop being a Goth person and start being a girl.

"I expect all this to start immediately. The wedding will be at the end of summer."

"Why?" I ask.

"Because that's when I could book Chalet Suzanne. They have a gazebo."

"No, I mean, why are you doing this? You're just going to divorce him too."

"Maybelline," my mother says sharply, "your negativity will give both you and me premature wrinkles. This time's for real. I can tell. Jake's a good man. He'll take care of us."

"Oh, I get it. We're not capable of taking care of ourselves, is that it?" I lower my voice. "Honestly, Chessy, we don't need Jake or any man."

My mother puts on her beauty queen smile. "Maybelline, every belle needs a beau."

"Gram didn't have a man around the house."

Chessy flinches and then shifts to her sweetest Southern drawl — the one she uses when she wants something. "I'd like you to be my maid of honor. I would have no one else but you, Maybelline."

She means no one else will do it. All Chessy's friends are men. Women don't trust her. I don't trust her. Last summer she went to the grocery store to get a cake for my sixteenth birthday but came home with Jake instead. He's the assistant manager at the Piggly Wiggly.

I never did get my cake.

"We'll do a supersized makeover and by the time I'm done, you'll look so good that no one will recognize you!" My mother returns to her normal voice. "Oh, and one more thing. You will not give me any more of your attitude. Is that clear?"

I flip her off.

"Come back here this instant," she yells. "Maybelline, come back!"

## ★ THREE ★

I like to be called Maybe, but my real name is Maybelline Mary Katherine Mary Ann Chestnut. Maybelline, after my mother's favorite brand of mascara. Mary Katherine, after Mary Katherine Campbell, the only person to be crowned Miss America twice. Mary Ann, after Mary Ann Mobley, an actress and a favorite Miss America of my mother's. And Chestnut, after Chessy's maiden name. I don't know my father's last name, or his first name either. I've asked, but my mother refuses to discuss it.

Ted is waiting for me at the corner. He's always waiting for me.

"Late again!"

"Drop it, Ted," I growl.

"I see," he says, shaking his head. "Princess didn't get enough of her beauty sleep. Am I right? Tell me I'm right. I'm always right."

"You're wrong." I start to tell him about my mother's latest engagement but stop midsentence. It's too early in the morning to talk about depressing stuff. Instead I snort, "Chessy thinks I'm Goth."

Ted bursts out laughing. "You? Goth?" he says as he repeatedly punches the WALK button. "What kind of Goth watches *Nelson's Neighborhood*?"

"Shut up!" I push him into the street.

As Ted and I near the high school, kids race past us. Still, we walk, even slowing our pace. I'm a library aide first period and Ms. Hodor doesn't care what time I get in as long as all the books get shelved. Ted works in the attendance office in the morning. They let him show up late because he can do the job of five students — six if he's had a Mountain Dew before school. He's so organized it's scary. Only, his grades suck. "That's because school bores me," Ted claims. "It's not challenging enough for someone as smart as me."

Ted and I have been best friends since the second week of our freshman year when he saw the Fantastic Five torment me. That's what they call themselves. How stupid is that? They are the prettiest, meanest, most popular girls, and if that's not bad enough, they all attend my mother's charm school. "You are my favorite girls in the entire world!" she's always telling them.

Where does that leave me?

So, flash back to freshman year. One of the Fantastic Five didn't even try to lower her voice when she said, "That Maybelline Chestnut, how is it that her mother's such a beauty and she's a beast?"

I hugged my backpack to my chest.

Out of nowhere, Ted charged up to them like a bull and boomed, *"Farang!"*

The girls just laughed, but you could tell they were confused. Plus this other geeky kid started filming the whole thing.

"*Farang!*" Ted shouted again and again. "*Farang! FARANG!*" Slowly, the Fantastic Five backed away and then started running and screaming and waving their arms in the air like you see people do in horror movies. It was awesome.

Later, I asked Ted what *farang* meant. "Foreigner," he told me. "I don't know any dirty words in Thai, but I'm working on it."

Ted's real name is Thammasat Tantipinichwong Schneider. He's adopted, which is instantly clear if you look at his family, who are all big and fat and freckly with carrot-colored hair. He's more than a head shorter than me, tanned, and so lightweight that I can carry him around on my back. Ted has obscenely long eyelashes, huge brown eyes that don't miss anything, and a mess of black hair that can't decide whether to lie flat or be curly. On Saturdays his parents drive him all the way over to Tampa, where there's a Thai Culture Club. There's not much Thai culture here in Kissimmee. There's not much culture, period.

Even though the second bell has rung, there are still students scurrying all over campus. Ms. Hodor nods to me when I finally walk into the library. I toss my backpack into the corner and head to the workroom, where the return bin is overflowing. If you don't return your library books by the end of the school year, you don't graduate. Hollywood has already started sorting. He's a senior and really tall and skinny. When he's bent over the library cart, his body looks like a question mark with an Afro, even though he's white. He straightens up when he sees me.

"Hi Maybe!"

"Hey Hollywood."

Hollywood pulls something out of his pocket. "Look!" It's his acceptance letter from the University of Southern California in Los Angeles. It has been Hollywood's life ambition to get into the USC film school. We've talked about it for hours. I even helped him write his essay. "I can't believe it's really happening," he says. "So I've decided not to let this letter out of my sight until I get there. John Carpenter, Sam Peckinpah, George Lucas, they all went to USC."

He breaks into an imitation of R2-D2 and I laugh, more at him acting all spazzed out than his imitation. Then he picks up his ancient Super 8 camera. "Maybe, smile!" Hollywood says. "I'm making a farewell film for myself."

I stare straight at the lens. Hollywood's always filming me and Ted. "Even though you're a major pain in the ass," I tell him, "I'm really going to miss you."

Hollywood lowers his camera. His voice cracks. "Really, Maybe?" He comes toward me with a funny look on his face. "Are you really going to miss me?"

"Whoa, cowboy," I say, holding up my hands. "I'm going to miss your weirdness, that's all."

Hollywood smiles. He has a crazy, crooked smile that makes him look like he's a little kid who's just done something wrong. "I'll take what I can get." Suddenly he's all twitchy. "Hey, want to go get dinner tonight?"

"Naw," I tell him. "I gotta head right home to help Chessy. There's a pageant coming up."

"Oh. Okay." He folds the letter carefully and puts it in his back pocket. "Some other time, then."

"Yeah, some other time."

I finish shelving the books and then head to Mr. Santat's art class, where I draw my hand, only it looks more like a claw. For

English we are assigned to read *The Member of the Wedding* by Carson McCullers. Ironic that Mrs. Nese would assign that book, considering the bombshell my mother has dropped this morning. When lunchtime rolls around, I ignore the Fantastic Five, then I zone out all through biology and most of the rest of my classes too.

Finally, school's over. It is sweltering outside, the temperature over one hundred degrees. Welcome to Florida in the summertime. As I head home, the clouds crack open — just on my side of the street. After fifteen minutes, it stops. Steam rises from the sidewalk.

There's no outside entrance to our apartment, so I am forced to walk through the charm school on the ground floor. One of the photos of old movie stars on Chessy's Wall of Beauty is crooked. I don't bother to straighten it. Chessy is in her office surrounded by newspaper clippings, crowns, and other relics from her beauty queen days.

"My God, Maybelline!" My mother stares at me. "You look like something from a horror movie. Move it before my girls see you. You're bad for business."

"Love you too," I say.

"Wait, what do you think of this?" she says as I turn to leave. Chessy holds up a sketch of a kimono and a swatch of blue silk. "This is for the Miss Greater Osceola Area Outstanding Teen Pageant — isn't it spectacular? And look at these!" She holds up even more drawings.

"They look like Halloween costumes."

"High ethnical standards are thirty-five percent of this pageant," my mother informs me.

"Ethnical standards?"

"It's a new category. I've commissioned Ridgeway to create special ethnically-correct dresses, but with rhinestones and sequins. It was hard talking the mothers into spending the extra money, but once I explained how it would give my girls an edge, everyone was all for it."

One of the services Chessy offers her students is beauty pageant coaching. She will do one-on-one training sessions and even accompany her girls to the contests. Chessy's got a reputation for training winners. For the past six years, the Fantastic Five have dominated every pageant they've entered.

My mother examines the blue silk and without looking up says, "Maybelline, we could start your makeover this weekend."

"Drop it," I moan.

She lets out a sigh. "What about a little diet? Jake could get us a case of SlimAway shakes. Then you wouldn't have to wear those men's T-shirts all the time to hide your fat. When I was your age . . ."

I can still hear Chessy blathering as I clomp up the stairs. When my mother was my age she was Miss Teen Dream. Chessy's always had this thing for crowns and goes royal on me all the time. She's the sole proprietor of Chessy Chestnut's Charm School for Young Ladies, aka CC's Charm School. Her slogan was "Be all that you can be!" until Upton Sinclair snorted, "That's a laugh! Don't you know that's the line the Army uses to recruit soldiers?" (He ought to know, he was an Army deserter.) Chessy had already had the slogan painted on the side of the building, so she made Carlos, soon-to-be husband number six, add, "And so much more!!!"

My mother was really somebody during her pageant circuit days. Some of her bigger titles include: Miss Silver Spurs Rodeo,

Miss Zellwood Corn Festival, Miss Plant City Strawberry Fest, Miss Kissimmee, Miss Osceola County, Miss Central Florida, Miss Florida. They say she could have been Miss America, except that when the time came for her to fly to Atlantic City for the pageant, she wigged out. It even made the newspaper: "Miss Florida Misses the Plane."

Upstairs, I stare into the mirror. I do look like a monster. My makeup is smudged, and the orange from my hair is dripping down my forehead. I wash everything off. My face looks blank without makeup, like nobody's home. I reapply my kohl eyeliner and deep purple lipstick, then change into a fresh black T-shirt.

I go back downstairs. "I'm eating at Ted's tonight," I tell Chessy.

"Good," she yells after me. "Jake's taking me bowling, so be sure to call before you come home."

★   ★   ★

I love it at Ted's house. Everyone there is normal. No one wears a crown and Ted's mom is never "on." His parents dote on Ted, like he's Baby Jesus or something. Maybe he is. Paww found him at the base of the statue of St. Anthony tucked into a shoebox with a book called *My Thai Baby* beside him. Two months later, in the presence of God, an adoption advocate, and a judge, the Schneiders swore to raise him, love him, and make sure he was in touch with his cultural heritage. His parents take this so seriously, they insist on being called Maah and Paww, the Thai equivalent of mother and father.

Maah hands me the chopsticks. "Can I spend the night?" I ask as I set the table. We're having pad Thai, my favorite. "Jake's taking my mother bowling."

"Chessy bowls?"

"Well, he bowls and she watches. She can't bowl on account of her acrylic nails."

"Of course you can stay here, Maybe. I even emptied one of the dresser drawers in the spare room for you." Maah gives me a hug. "You are welcome here anytime, darling. You're family."

Sure enough, on the second dresser drawer is a label that reads: MAYBE'S ONLY. I open it and smile when I see a brand-new toothbrush and a tube of toothpaste waiting for me. Next, I wander down the hall. Ted's walls are plastered with photos of Thailand. A poster touting Sunthorn Phu Day is on his closet door. There's a Thai flag above his bed, near the autographed photo of Yo-Yo Ma, the cellist. On his dresser rests a small shrine to Buddha with fresh flowers around it.

"Maybe — supper's on!" Paww calls out.

Maah's cooking is divine. We never have home-cooked meals at my house. Chessy and I are both pretty good at the electric can opener, though.

After dinner, Paww and Maah snuggle on the couch. I claim the love seat and Ted curls up in the rocking chair. He tosses the remote to his dad, then we all settle in for another Friday night of television.

## ★ FOUR ★

**C**hessy and Jake are probably back from bowling. I can only imagine what they're doing. The walls at home are pretty thin.

Jake Himmler. Chessy's really scraping the bottom of the barrel this time. He likes to brag that he started working at Piggly Wiggly when he was in high school and never left. Jake wooed my mother with cases of toilet paper, boxes of oranges, and tubs of margarine — things he stole from the grocery store. Once, when I called him on it, Jake said, "Perks, Maybelline. Perks of the job." He looked me up and down and added, "I work hard, so why shouldn't I get a little something extra?"

You've heard of serial murderers? My mother's a serial marryer. It's a disease. The husbands get blinded by the big blonde hair and big boobs and big personality. There's so much big stuff that they never notice the little cracks in the marriage until it's too late. She married, in order:

1) *Mark Abajian* — full-time mechanic and part-time bodybuilder, honeymoon: Gainesville, Florida, divorced

after sixteen months, "He came between me and my dreams" (he wanted her to give up the Charm School)

2) *Sammy Wing* — photographer, honeymoon: Miami, Florida, divorced after eight months, "He didn't love me for who I was" (he wanted her to give up drinking)

3) *Jim Marshall* — banker, honeymoon: Amelia Island, Florida, divorced after three months, "He was boring" (he wouldn't go dancing with her)

4) *Sammy Wing* — photographer, honeymoon: St. Augustine, Florida, divorced after three years, "He was selfish" (his career took him to California and she refused to move)

5) *Upton Sinclair* — U.S. military, retired, honeymoon: Clearwater, Florida, divorced after eight months, "He wasn't who he said he was" (that's true)

6) *Carlos Alvarez* — sign painter, honeymoon: Key West, Florida, divorced after fifty-four hours, "He was trying to ruin my life" (he wanted a baby).

My favorite of all her husbands was Sammy Wing. He took the only picture of me that I don't hate. In it, I don't look angry or mad. I just look, I dunno. I don't look like me. I look normal. Like a normal girl. If you didn't know it was me, you'd think, "Oh, she's a regular person. Probably has nice parents, lots of friends, a good life."

The second time Chessy and Sammy married I was convinced it would stick, and it did for three whole years, from when I was seven to ten. That's when Sammy took that good photo of me. He also got Chessy to cut back on her drinking and promised her he'd look after me. Sammy had big plans. We were going to move to California and he was going to adopt me, but instead my mom and Sammy got divorced.

Did Sammy know, I wonder? Did any of them know what they were getting into, or how lucky they were to get out? There's one man who's not on that list but should be. Maybe the only man Chessy's ever met who didn't want to marry her. That would be my father. I guess he was smarter than the rest of them.

My mother has done an excellent job at erasing all traces of my biological father. She refuses to discuss him, although she has let a couple things slip. Like that he was some bigwig working on a television show based in Florida, and he thought she was beautiful. Once during one of our fights I yelled, "Well then, I'm going to go live with my real dad."

"I'd like to see you try," she said, laughing. "He doesn't even know you're alive."

I was about to swat her in the head with a loaf of bread but stopped myself. "What?"

"I told him you died," she said smugly. "Told him I had a miscarriage."

"You told him I *died*?" I hugged the bread so tight I flattened it.

She sobered up for a moment and with a voice thick with regret said, "Maybelline, he didn't want me either. He made that clear when he went back to Los Angeles. Besides, he said he never wanted kids."

That's the closest mother-daughter-father bonding experience we've ever had.

I turn over in bed and face the wall in the Schneiders' spare room. The ceiling fan is on. It chugs away like it wants me to know how hard it's working. Still, I barely feel it.

I have a folder that I keep in my T-shirt drawer. It's filled with magazine photos of movie and TV directors and producers. Who knows? One of them might be my father. I wonder what he's doing right now?

I wonder who he is?

What he looks like?

What he does for a living?

I wonder if he'd want to know about me?

I'm sure he would. Imagine, going all this time not knowing you had a daughter.

Would he want to know?

I wonder.

## ★ FIVE ★

It's only been a week since I heard the news about my mother's latest engagement, but I'm already starting to see disturbing changes. Bowling trophies compete with pageant trophies in the living room. A worn leather chair sprouting fluff from the armrest has been plopped down in the center of the room. It faces the giant television Jake installed in the corner. There's a very complicated remote control, but it's unnecessary. The TV stays on bowling 24/7.

Jake is over here now. His bowling shirt is open, revealing a beer belly. He looks pregnant. "Chessy darlin', you're a 300 if there ever was one," Jake says, winking and raising his Bud Light. My mother eats this up. Tell her she's pretty and she'll marry you.

I take the cheese from the fridge and sniff it. It smells bad, but there's not much else to eat. I slap it between two slices of bread.

"Who ate all the bologna?" I ask, looking back in the living room.

"Sorry, Daughter," Jake says. I know my biological father is a thousand times classier than the man who's about to become husband number seven.

"I'm not your daughter," I inform him.

"Soon enough," he says, this time winking at me. I try not to throw up.

Chessy ignores this whole exchange. She's engrossed in the pages of *BRIDES*. My mom has a lifetime subscription to the magazine. As she turns the pages, she says to no one, "Ridgeway will create a Vera Wang–style wedding dress for me. Genuine Swarovski crystals will be nestled in my hair. The wedding cake will be nothing less than a four-tiered pumpkin chocolate chip with ivory fondant and buttercream icing. . . ."

Crazy as it sounds, this is nothing compared to her other weddings. The only thing stopping my mother from going overboard this time is the upcoming Miss Greater Osceola Area Outstanding Teen Pageant. Chessy approaches weddings and pageants with the same wild-eyed zeal, like a deranged animal on the hunt.

I can't wait for both of them to be over — the pageant so I don't have to hear about the ethnical competition anymore, and the wedding so she can hurry up and divorce Jake and get him out of my life. He's creepy. The Fantastic Five come over every evening to practice for the pageant. Sometimes Jake watches them rehearse, never taking his eyes off them. He seems to enjoy this a little more than he should.

The buzzer goes off downstairs. Chessy quickly closes her magazine and rushes downstairs to her wards. I sit at the top of the stairs and peer down through the banister. No one can see me. For years I've sat up here and watched my mother and her girls.

As they await Ridgeway's arrival, the Fantastic Five recite Chessy's Seven Select Rules for Young Ladies:

1) Offer a fabulous first impression — for a lasting impression!

2) Strike a perfect pose — to keep you on your toes!

3) Train your talent — reap your rewards!

4) Develop magical makeup artistry — and make them look twice!

5) Wear a winning wardrobe — project a winning attitude!

6) Put forth savvy speech and presence — and create a sensational personality!

7) And so much more!

When they're done, Chessy gushes, "You girls are amazing. I can only imagine how beautiful you will look in Ridgeway's creations."

On cue, Ridgeway makes his entrance, pushing a rack of gorgeous dresses. There is a chorus of *oohs* and *aahs* as everyone tries on the ethnical costumes he has custom-designed for them.

"Ladies, ladies, please stop jumping up and down like critters at the Gatorland Jump-a-Roo." Ridgeway's faux Australian accent drips with sarcasm. "How can I make sure these all fit properly?"

Ridgeway is the best. His gowns can fetch up to twelve hundred dollars each, but he always gives a deep discount to "Chessy's Charmers," as she's branded them. I think they deserve to be branded, just like the cattle that graze near the Piggly Wiggly.

I wish my mom would marry Ridgeway. They share a love of old movies, bias-cut beaded gowns, and business. I've heard her say, "Ridgeway, you are my one true friend." The only problem is, he's got his heart set on Brock Rivers, the actor from that cheesy cowboy series set in Australia. "If it's not Brock, then it's nobody," Ridgeway sighs.

So it's nobody.

I have to go downstairs to get something from the office. As I brush past the Fantastic Five one of them says, "Look, it's the beast!" Someone else adds, "Her hair is green today. She's not a beast, she's a troll."

"You could use more concealer, Maybelline," another one says. "Like over your entire body."

As usual, my mother pretends not to hear them, even though their laughter echoes in the building.

Ridgeway jabs one of them with a straight pin as he adjusts her costume.

"Ouch!"

"Oh dear. So sorry," he says, winking at me.

I smile and keep walking, face forward, head up high, and don't stop until I get upstairs. I should be used to their abuse by now. It's been going on forever. One time I thought my mother was going to reprimand them, but instead she said, "Maybelline, stop distracting everyone."

There's not much in the fridge. Some SlimAway shakes. Diet soda. Nail polish. Then I spy something I can use.

I head back downstairs. No one pays any attention to me. They're too busy admiring themselves in their ethnical costumes. The Fantastic Five's Pretty Pageant tote bags are all in one corner. One by one, I open each bag and squeeze mustard into them until I've run out. There will be hell to pay later, but it'll be worth it.

**M**aybe, you're a diabolical genius!"

At lunch on Monday, Ted makes me tell him about the mustard over and over and laughs just as hard every time. "This rivals the time you painted 'I am stoopid' on their lockers," he howls. "But not quite as good as that time you replaced their hairspray with bug spray." He starts laughing all over again.

Hollywood comes over and sits with us. "What's so funny?"

"Nothing," I say. Ted and I try not to crack up as we continue eating our spring rolls. Maah has even included a small container with homemade peanut sauce for dipping.

Hollywood opens a paper bag. "What's in there?" Ted asks, pointing to a giant sandwich.

"Everything," Hollywood says, taking a bite. "I just put in whatever I could find." He talks with his mouth full. "See, some cheese, some chips, a fried egg." Hollywood puts down his sandwich, picks up his camera, and starts filming.

When Hollywood first told me, "I want to make movies," I thought he was delusional. Then he showed us some of his films.

Ted sat still without talking for the entire forty-five minutes — a new world record. When the lights came back on, Ted poked me and whispered, "Hollywood's amazing."

"Yeah," I whispered back. "I had no idea he was so talented. He doesn't belong here."

I put my hand up in front of Hollywood's camera. "Enough, college boy," I tell him. "Why don't you shoot someone else for a change?"

Hollywood sputters defensively, "I film other people too."

"You could film me more," Ted offers. "I'm very photogenic."

The warning bell rings. I head to the bathroom. It's empty. Good. I hate it when people are in there and I have to pee. Usually the bathroom is full of girls putting on their makeup, or doing their hair, or just hanging out. Who would want to hang out in a bathroom?

I flush the toilet and the lights go out. Just my luck. There are no windows so it's totally dark. I open the stall door and step out. Someone laughs. I freak. The lights go on and I go down. I am fighting, but there are too many of them. I scream. Someone shoves something in my mouth and orders me to shut up. Several pin me to the floor, but I get some good kicks and punches in. I'm pretty strong for someone who never works out.

The second bell rings and they race out of the bathroom. The last one to leave turns off the lights. I am lying on the floor. My head hurts. I am having trouble breathing. I lie still and listen to students stampeding to class until there is silence. I shut my eyes. Maybe I'll just stay here all day. No one will notice that I'm missing.

There are footsteps again. They are getting closer. The door opens. It's the principal. She always checks the bathroom to make sure no one's ditching class.

"Oh my God," Mrs. Escobar yells. "Oh my God! Maybelline, what happened? Who did this to you?"

I remove the maxi pad from my mouth. She helps me up. I see myself in the mirror and start to scream.

"I'll call 911," she says, pulling out her walkie-talkie.

"No, no, it's okay," I assure her.

"But . . . but you're all bloody," she stammers.

"Lipstick," I say. "It's lipstick."

"Lipstick?"

"Lipstick."

As she escorts me to her office, I spy Hollywood across the courtyard with his camera. Shouldn't he be in class?

I've been to the principal's office many times before. For cutting school. For destroying public property. For my attitude. Only this time, Mrs. Escobar is being nice to me. Her brow is furrowed. She hands me her tissue box. I try wiping the lipstick off my face as Mrs. Escobar taps a pencil on her desk. Finally she asks, "Who did this to you, Maybelline?"

"I don't know."

"You do know."

"No I don't."

Mrs. Escobar lets out a long sigh. "You do know who did this, and I don't know why you would protect them."

"May I go? I don't want to be late for English."

I rise, but Mrs. Escobar signals for me to sit down. She opens up a file. "You're a good student and you score well on tests," she says as she flips through the pages. "If you clean up your act, I can get rid of this stuff on your record. Next year you'll be a senior. Are you thinking of college?"

"I'm not college material," I say dully, repeating something that Chessy's told me many times.

A flicker of disapproval crosses her face. "I think you are. Mrs. Nese does too. She's told me that you have potential. You should go. It'll open doors for you."

"I really don't want to be late to class. . . ."

Mrs. Escobar sighs. "You're excused, Maybelline."

## ★ SEVEN ★

It's all over campus that I was attacked in the girls' bathroom. The rumors range from kids from a rival school to the substitute biology teacher who wears a belt and suspenders.

"You have to turn them in," Ted insists.

"Drop it. I'm not finking."

"Why not? They'll get suspended for sure. We have to do this!"

"*We* don't have to do anything. There are only a couple days of school left, so suspension is no big deal. Besides, if I turn them in they may quit the Charm School, and then living with Chessy will be even more hell than it already is. Plus we need the money. There's another wedding coming up, remember?"

"I thought your mom had money," Ted says as we walk past the cafeteria. I try not to look at all the kids trying not to look at me.

"Had money, Ted. Had."

We've gone into debt every time Chessy's gotten married. A couple of her husbands made a lot of money, like Sammy Wing, the photographer, and Jim Marshall, the banker. But when they left, so did the nice lifestyle. Upton Sinclair spent a ton of money on my mother. He even bought me my own TV. Later we found out the credit cards he used weren't his. When Chessy kicked him out, not only did he take the TV back, he helped himself to her jewelry and did an excellent job at cleaning out her bank account.

Hollywood is walking toward us, his Super 8 aimed at me. "Maybe, can you tell me about the attack in the bathroom?"

"Shut that stupid thing off," I bark.

Hollywood looks hurt. He's always getting all emotional on me.

"Don't feel bad," Ted consoles him. "Maybe's still humiliated that she got beat up. Plus she has raging PMS."

I pinch Ted's arm.

Hollywood shoves his camera into his beat-up backpack. "You guys want a ride home?" he asks.

"You know it, big guy!" Ted says. He has to jump to high-five Hollywood.

One of Hollywood's most admirable traits is that he has a car. Whenever Ted and I want to go somewhere, we know we can count on him. The downside is that he has to come with us. Hollywood's okay, I guess. He's always around, sort of like a rash that you get used to after a while.

I ride shotgun. Ted stretches out in the backseat as Hollywood folds himself into the driver's side. The car is an ancient Toyota. The green paint is peeling off and even the rust has seen better days. Hollywood's named his car the Green Hornet, after some old television show. There's no air conditioning and the radio only works some of the time. A laminated photo of James Dean is stapled to the dashboard.

"*Rebel Without a Cause* is one of the best films ever made," Hollywood says. He tells us this every time we get into his car.

"Isn't it kind of gay to have a photo of James Dean?" asks Ted.

Hollywood turns red. "No," he says evenly. "James Dean's a great actor. Very understated. *Giant, Rebel, East of Eden*, he only made three films, but each revealed his genius. . . ."

As he blabbers on, I wonder if Hollywood is gay. He's never had a girlfriend, or even gone out with a girl, except for that disastrous blind date during spring break. But who am I to talk? I've only had one quasi boyfriend in my entire life. I met Ryan last summer at the Dairy Queen near his family's vacation rental on Lake Tohopekaliga. All we did was make out, but he left me after three weeks because I didn't put out. I seriously considered it, but ultimately decided that I didn't want Ryan to see my body. I was afraid he'd laugh.

Chessy's always harping at me: "Maybelline, if you'd just lose some weight, wear proper makeup, stop coloring your hair with Kool-Aid, and shed those baggy Goth-boy clothes, you'd be able to snag a boyfriend."

What makes her think I'd even want a boyfriend? There's more to life than boys. Or men. Or husbands.

As the Green Hornet pulls up in front of CC's Charm School, the car burps to a stop. Hollywood looks like he wants to say something.

"What?" I ask.

"I dunno. It's just that I'm graduating tomorrow, and then I leave for California. I'm taking screenwriting at USC for summer school so I can get a jump on college." He runs his fingers over James Dean's photo and lets out a troubled sigh.

"I'd think you'd be happier," Ted says from the backseat. "You're graduating. You're going to the school of your dreams. You're getting out of Kissimmee."

"I am happy," Hollywood says unconvincingly. "I don't know. I've never been out of Florida, and now I'm driving across the country to a place I've never been to before? I may never see you two again." He looks right at me when he says this.

I roll my eyes. "Oh, please, don't go all drama queen on me."

Hollywood is quiet. He gets moody. Last summer he wouldn't even speak to me.

"Hello? There is such a thing as a telephone," Ted says.

"You know I don't have a cell phone."

"Well, I do and you can call me on mine, okay?" Ted pats him reassuringly on the shoulder. "Anytime is fine with me. I never turn my phone off. Never."

"The only person who ever calls you is your mother," I point out.

"So," Ted huffs. "That could change."

"Hollywood, you gotta go," I say. "My mother's never left Florida and look what happened to her."

"What if I fail?" Hollywood moans. He buries his face in his hands.

"You won't," I insist. "Jesus, Hollywood, you've got talent. You're going to be famous."

"I don't know. He might bomb," Ted muses. "Competition is really tough in filmmaking. Do you know how hard it is to get a movie produced? You have a better chance at being struck by lightning than having a hit film."

Hollywood slumps back like he's been shot. "What am I doing?"

"You're doing what you've always wanted to do." I swat Ted in the head.

"Ouch!"

"Suck it up, Hollywood," I tell him. "Remember all those late-night talks we had about what you'd do if you ever got out of Kissimmee? Make us proud." I open the car door and we all get out. Hollywood gives me a hug and won't let go. "You weirdo," I laugh as I push him away.

"Hey, what about me?" Ted asks.

I reach over toward Ted. "Not you, him!" Ted says, grabbing Hollywood and giving him a bear hug.

Ted and I watch him drive off. Exhaust pours out of the car as it backfires.

"I don't know if that pitiful thing is going to make it all the way to Los Angeles," Ted comments.

"It is pretty old." I nod.

"Not the Green Hornet." Ted shakes his head. "I meant Hollywood."

## ★ EIGHT ★

**M**y mother is giddy. The Miss Greater Osceola Area Outstanding Teen Pageant is today. "Ridgeway's ethnical dresses will give us the edge," she says as she depletes the ozone by adding yet another layer of hairspray to her already lacquered head. Chessy has pre-reserved a space in the *Kissimmee Gazette*. She always says, "If you want them to take notice, take out an ad."

*Congratulations to*
*Miss Greater Osceola Area*
*Outstanding Teen Pageant winner*
(insert name and photo)
*from CC's Charm School.*
**You too can be a winner.**
**Learn to be a model, actress, or pageant princess,**
**or just make everyone think you are one!**
**Be all that you can be, and more at 20% off with this ad.**

She also gives free first lessons and a discount to returning students. But her best advertisements are when the Fantastic Five win.

After Chessy's gone, I open the window. With so much hair spray and Shalimar hanging in the air, our apartment is a fire hazard.

It's nice to have the place to myself. I sink into Jake's big leather chair and grab the remote. The KidVid channel is featuring a *Nelson's Neighborhood* marathon. I love *Nelson's Neighborhood*. It's been in reruns for the past five years or so, but I watch it every day. It's about this contemporary family who act really retro, all straightlaced and everything. There are the twins (a girl and a boy), the parents, and their loyal dog, Chipper. Together they have all these cool adventures, like the time they went camping and Chipper got lost and was mauled by a bear — and it brought them all closer together.

I am totally in love with Christian Culver, who plays Nelson B. Nelson, the sensitive, Shakespeare-reading, guitar-playing son who rescues baby animals and is an Olympic diving hopeful. Even though I've resolved never to get married, I'd say "I do" to him in a heartbeat.

It's around six P.M. I can't believe I've watched over nine hours of *Nelson's Neighborhood*. I finish off the mint Oreos, then call out for a pizza and consider having a beer. Now that Jake's around, the fridge is full of them. Chessy prefers her booze room temperature. The last time I drank I got really sick. The only person worse off than me was Ted. "Asians excel at everything but alcohol," he explained between heaves.

My mother can hold her liquor pretty well. It comes from years of practice. However, once she passes the three-drink mark she starts to get stupid. After four she's blotto, and after five she's worthless. On occasion she completely blacks out — usually toward the end of a marriage.

I reach toward the beers and move them aside, grabbing a Dr. Pepper in the back. Big-screen television. Leather chair. Pizza. Soda. *Nelson's Neighborhood*. This is heaven.

Was I sleeping? I wake up thinking I'm in France. "*Voilà la porte, mes amies*," a woman is shouting. "I learned to speak French fluently in less than a week!"

Oh. It's just that stupid infomercial. I turn the volume down when I hear noises downstairs. Chessy must be home. Voices rise. There is shouting. Glass shatters. I tiptoe to the stairs and peer down into the Charm School. My mother is sitting on the floor speaking gibberish. Her legs splay out like a rag doll. Her crystal Best Teen Smile award is in pieces.

"Should we call a doctor?" Ridgeway asks. He is holding a broom.

"No, we'll just get some booze into her and let her sleep it off," Jake says. He goes into Chessy's office and pulls a bottle of whiskey out of her file cabinet. "Here, hon," he says, handing it to her. "Your friend Jack Daniels is gonna make you feel a whole lot better."

I wince. Jack Daniels is no friend of hers. Chessy's hysterical, but she does what she's told. I've seen enough. I sneak back into the apartment.

Later, Jake and Ridgeway help my mother up the stairs and lead her into the bedroom. Now she's laughing and singing a medley of Broadway show tunes.

Ridgeway comes back into the living room once Chessy is tucked in. "It wasn't an 'ethnical' competition," he says dryly. He helps himself to a slice of my cold pizza. "It was 'ethical'; they wanted the girls to have high ethical values and to demonstrate it by giving a speech or some sort of presentation."

"Oh my God!" I cover my mouth. When I can't hold it in any longer I burst out laughing. Ridgeway joins me and soon we are in tears.

He dabs his eyes with his handkerchief. "Oh, darling, this really isn't funny. The girls are so upset. They're humiliated. Their mothers have threatened to pull them all out of the Charm School. When word about this gets out, Chessy's going to be the laughingstock of the pageant circuit."

I take a deep breath. I know he's right. Still, I wish I could have been there.

Ridgeway gets up. "I'd better go. Jake will take care of your mom. She's going to be pretty hard to live with for a while."

What an understatement.

For a change, I'm glad Jake's here.

It's early, but I'm tired. I go to bed.

# ★ NINE ★

I am asleep and dreaming that James Dean is making the moves on me. He's not the good-looking James Dean in Hollywood's photo. He's an old and bloated James Dean with really bad breath.

I push him away, but he keeps coming at me. He is relentless. Suddenly I am awake. I try to sit up, but someone pushes me down. I smell beer.

It's not James Dean. It's Jake.

I'm not sure what's happening.

"Get off of me!"

"Quiet," he slurs. "You'll wake your mother."

One hand is groping under my T-shirt and the other is moving up my leg. He starts to pull my shorts down and press against me. I shove him hard and he rolls onto the floor. But he just keeps coming back, again and again. He slaps me and covers my mouth, then slobbers in my ear, "Who's your daddy now?"

I bite his hand hard.

"God damn it!" Spit flies from his mouth as he shouts. I curl up in a ball and grip my pillow, but that doesn't stop him. He's all over me. I'm fighting, but he's winning.

"Get away!" I scream.

The lights go on.

It's Chessy.

"Oh my Lord, I don't believe this."

Jake and I both freeze. For once I am happy to see my mother.

"I can explain," he starts to say. Jake stumbles as he gets out of the bed. His stomach hangs over his boxers. He's not wearing a shirt.

"I don't need any explanations," she says coldly. She looks at Jake, then me. Her eyes narrow.

"Maybelline, I can't believe you would do this to me."

My throat makes a strangled sound, but I can't find any words. Chessy's arms are folded across her chest. Her glare slices through me.

"But Mom," I whimper.

"But nothing."

I pull the sheet up to my chin. My face is wet. I am crying.

Jake follows her into the kitchen.

"I'm sorry you had to see that, baby," he murmurs, still loud enough for me to hear. "But that kid of yours is no angel. She's been making passes at me since the first time we met. She called me into her room. Said she needed help with something —"

"Don't you talk to me," Chessy snaps. "I thought you loved me."

"Oh baby, I do love you," he says. "Come here. Come here."

"Jake, how could you two do this to me?" she wails. "You tramp!" she shouts in my direction. "You're nothing but trouble. I wish I'd never had you."

While Jake and my mother argue in the kitchen, I quickly get dressed and slip out of the house.

I know one thing.

I'm never going back.

## ★ TEN ★

I walk for hours before ringing the doorbell. Maah doesn't act surprised to see me at three A.M. "Hi, Maybe." She yawns as she steps aside to let me in. Her head is full of pink curlers. "Your mom drinking again?"

I just nod and head to the spare room. I crawl into bed without bothering to wash up or take off my jeans. Even though it's hot, I pull the covers over myself. Still, I can't stop shivering.

"Why did you even have me?" I once asked Chessy.

When she's drunk, Chessy blinks really slowly and men think she's coming on to them. Maybe she is.

"So I'd have someone to talk to," my mother slurred as she cradled her bottle of Jack Daniels like a baby.

I don't want to talk to her ever again.

In the morning I wake up to the sound of Paww calling out, "All sleepyheads, it's time for breakfast. I'm making flapjacks!"

Flapjacks! I love Paww's flapjacks. I'm happy until I try to get out of bed. My entire body is sore. Then I remember what happened last night. I take a long shower and dry off. As I get dressed I notice the bruises on my body. I take off my clothes and get back into the shower. I scrub and scrub. Still the bruises, and the memories, won't wash away.

After breakfast Ted and I walk along the train tracks. He is trying to balance on the railroad ties. I try too, but keep falling off. So instead, I pick up rocks and throw them into the bushes. Ted is blathering on and on about the five fundamental flavors of Thai food. When he gets going on a topic there's no stopping him.

"Ted —"

"Sweet, sour —"

"Ted —"

"Bitter, spicy —"

"Ted, Jake tried to rape me."

That got his attention. "WHAT? Maybe, are you okay? Did he hurt you? He didn't hurt you, did he? I'll kill him if he hurt you."

Ted's worried look breaks my heart.

"I'm okay."

"Does Chessy know?"

I toss another rock. "She thinks I came on to him."

"That's insane!"

"I know. And get this, he actually said, 'Who's your daddy now?' It was so disgusting!"

"He said that?"

"Twice."

"Did you call the police?"

I shake my head. "Who would believe me? My own mother doesn't even believe me."

"So what are you going to do?"

"I don't know. It was already torture before Jake showed up. Now it would be impossible to stay."

"What if she dumps him?"

"Get real. Like Chessy would ever call off a wedding. She's already sent out the invites. I don't matter to her anyway. I never did." I pick up another rock and throw it as hard as I can. "I'm thinking of living with my father."

"Which one?"

"My biological father."

"No way!" Ted stops walking and stares at me.

"Yeah, I've actually been thinking about this for a long time, even before this Jake thing. Ted, I'm going to try to find him."

"But I thought he doesn't even know you exist?"

"Well, if I find him he will."

Ted looks unsure. I start talking louder as if that will convince him it's a good idea. Or is it me I'm trying to convince? "He deserves to know he has a daughter. Ted, I may be half Chessy, but I gotta believe that there's someone else out there that I take after — someone better than her. I just want to meet him, not glom on to him or anything. I just want to meet him. Is that asking too much?" I'm crying. "Ted, I'm going to Los Angeles to find him. Will you go with me? Please, Ted. Please."

A range of expressions cross Ted's face as he processes my request. More than once, he opens his mouth to say something, and then shuts it. I hold my breath. Finally, he lets out a snort then breaks into a weary smile. "Okay, Maybe. Okay, I'll go."

I let out a whoop and Ted gives me a hug. Immediately, he starts making plans. "You'll need to go through all of Chessy's things and find some clues, like on that show, *America's Most Missing*."

"Chessy's pretty much in denial that he even existed," I say, wiping my tears with the back of my hand. "She won't have anything of his."

"Wake up, Sleeping Beauty. Your mother's a hopeless romantic —"

"She is hopeless," I mutter.

Ted ignores me. "Chessy's sure to have kept something from your father." He has a point. "Also, we'll need money. Los Angeles isn't cheap."

"I've got some money," I tell him. "I've been saving up for this, just in case."

"Well, I've got some money from investments," Ted adds. "And when we get to Los Angeles, we'll get our own place and jobs!"

We're both hopping around. This is wonderful!

"What will you tell Chessy?" he asks. This brings me crashing down.

"Nothing," I mumble. "I'll just disappear and see if she even notices. What'll you tell your parents?"

"I'll tell them that you're running away and I am going to be your chaperone." Ted pauses. "And I'll tell them that Los Angeles has a large Thai population and I'll be studying my culture while I'm there, sort of like a foreign exchange program." He stops and looks up in the air for inspiration, then adds, "And I will tell them that we are staying with your cousin Carla."

"I don't have a cousin Carla."

"It's a cover. A ruse. A lie, okay? Sheesh, how dense are you?"

My heart races. I can already envision finding my father. He will be surprised at first, then happy. We will both be happy.

"We just have to figure out how to get to Los Angeles," Ted muses.

"Hellooo," I say, waving a hand in front of his face. "Have you already forgotten how we've gotten around town all these years?"

Ted's face lights up. "The Green Hornet!"

I nod. "Hellooo, Hollywood!"

## ELEVEN

**H**ollywood can't stop grinning when we tell him.

"Are you kidding me? Are you kidding? You have got to be kidding!"

"We are not kidding, we are going to carpool," Ted says again. "Except we don't have a car."

"Hot damn," Hollywood shouts. "Road trip!"

★ ★ ★

Later that afternoon, I sneak back home. My mother's at her weekly beauty shop appointment. Jake's at work, but his stuff's still here. I don't know if he's coming back and I don't care. I gather my money and help myself to three hundred fifty bucks from the stash Chessy keeps in a coffee can under her bed. I also help myself to her old wedding rings. They might be worth something after all.

Next I rummage through the hatbox in her closet. Sitting on top is a snapshot of her parents before their divorce. Chessy must have been about four when that photo was taken. She's standing between her mother and father and no one looks happy. I move on to the mushy letters from every man she ever married, and quite a few from men she didn't. This surprises me. I thought she got hitched to everyone she's ever dated.

As I dig through old brochures and random notes, I'm about to give up when I come across a photo tucked inside a Christmas card. The picture is dated nine months before I was born. I take a sharp breath and stare at the photo. Underneath a sign that says ALLIGATOR ALLEY, a beautiful blonde clings to a man with dark hair and an uneasy smile. He's wearing a baseball cap and sunglasses, so it's hard to tell what he really looks like. On the back of the photo in Chessy's flowery handwriting is "Gunnar and me," surrounded by hearts.

He's got to be my father.

Carefully I tuck the photo back into the envelope and slip it into the "Father" folder in my duffel bag, alongside my clothes, makeup, and *On the Road* by Jack Kerouac. Before I go, I write Chessy a long letter explaining all the reasons why I'm running away. Then I tear it up and just say:

> *Going to live with Ted this summer in Los Angeles with his cousin Carla. Hollywood's driving.*
>
> — *Maybe*

I leave the note in the liquor cabinet, where I know she'll be sure to find it.

## ★ TWELVE ★

After being trapped for two days in the Green Hornet with Ted and Hollywood, I am ready to walk to California.

Ted had the full blessing of his parents, who were excited to see their boy explore his Thai culture, be independent, and "spread his wings and fly" — as long as he promised to call them twice a day. They armed him with an ATM card for emergencies, two letters of reference (one for the Thai community in Los Angeles, the other for potential employers), and a cooler filled with Thai delicacies and Dr. Pepper, Ted's beverage of choice.

Hollywood's family gave him a graduation/going away party and presented him with a sports jacket that was slightly too big — "in case I grow," he explained. His parents also gave him a promise that they would send money whenever they could. Hollywood's family lives in a trailer park. The beat-up double-wide is for Hollywood and his five siblings, the smaller trailer next door is for his mom and dad. Despite living apart, his family is really close.

I doubt if Chessy has noticed I'm gone. She's probably too busy with her wedding plans to think of anything else.

We decide that to save money we will sleep in the car. This morning, we woke up to three scary-looking guys demanding money and drugs. Since we didn't have either, one of them punched Hollywood. Any other person would have been humiliated, but Hollywood filmed his lip swelling up.

"People pay a lot of money for lips like yours," Ted said as he examined Hollywood's face. "That puffy look is very popular right now."

Hollywood started laughing but had to stop because it hurt.

It's starting to smell pretty ripe in the Toyota. The air conditioning is busted and we're all hot and sweaty. Plus, we just throw the garbage in the backseat, which really pisses Ted off because it always lands on him.

After the drugs/swelled-lip incident, we cough up the cash to check into a motel outside of San Antonio. The sign says free Internet access. Too bad none of us has a computer. The bathroom smells musty. Still, it feels great to take a shower and I stay in there until Ted starts banging on the door. "Hurry up, Maybe. We're hungry!"

As we walk down a dirt road, Ted shuffles his feet and kicks up dust. "Stop that!" I yell. "I just got clean." When he ignores me, I shove him. He head butts me and I fall down. "Ted, I'm going to kill you!" I shout as I lunge at him.

When Hollywood tries to break up our fight Ted tackles him. Soon they're wrestling. Hollywood's so much bigger than Ted, but Ted has speed.

"Stop it, you guys," I shout. "I'm hungry!"

"Me too," Ted says, grinning from the headlock Hollywood has him in.

There's only one waitress at Marie's Coffee Shop.

"Is Marie here?" Hollywood asks. Only his lip is still swollen, so it sounds like he's said, "Eth Mar-wee ear?" The waitress stares at us like she's never seen a white boy with an Afro, a Thai boy with slicked-up hair, and a Goth girl with pink hair.

The restaurant is practically empty except for two elderly men in overalls sitting at the counter. I wonder if they are twins. Neither speaks, instead they just stare straight ahead and chew in unison. And she thinks we're strange?

I order breakfast even though it's past dinnertime — eggs over easy, French toast, sausage, and orange juice. Ted asks the waitress about each item on the menu.

"Will the chili give me gas?"

"Do the string beans come from a can?"

"Is the homemade pie homemade?"

In the end he gets two hamburgers with extra pickles and fries. Hollywood makes a big deal about shutting his eyes and pointing at the menu.

While we're waiting for our food, Ted whips out his cell phone. "Hi Maah! Yeah, I miss you too. How's Paww? Oh my God! Is he okay? Did the bull get him?" Paww is a rodeo clown. "Good . . . Okay, yeah. Well you scared me! Yeah, she's here. Wait." Ted looks at me. "Maah says hi." I wave to the phone. Ted must talk to his parents five times a day. "Hi Paww, I'm glad you're okay. I love you too. Okay. Bye." In the Schneider house they say, "I love you" as often as Chessy said, "Maybelline, you're an embarrassment."

Ted's always happy after he's talked to his parents. "The first summer I spent away from home, I was eight," he says, reaching for the ketchup. He douses his French fries and then pours an obscene amount of salt over them. There's a cracker in the saltshaker. "I was at Thai Buddies sleepover camp and I didn't get homesick once, but Maah later told me she cried everyday I was gone."

"My mom started crying on the day I got my scholarship to USC," Hollywood says. It's getting easier for me to understand him. He stops filming his dinner and pokes at his liver and onions with his fork. "She's probably still crying."

"My mother's never cried over me," I recall.

Hollywood eyes my French toast. "Do you want to trade?"

I switch plates. I'm not hungry.

As Ted and Hollywood debate their Top Ten favorite films, I look down at the liver and onions. I hate liver and onions.

"You can't list *Willy Wonka* twice!" Hollywood protests.

"You can't keep naming movies no one's ever heard of!" Ted says, stabbing Hollywood in the arm with a French fry. "How do I even know if they're real?"

When we get back to the motel, the three of us stare at the two beds. They are twin-sized.

"I get one because I'm doing all the driving," Hollywood announces. He takes off his shirt. When I try to avert my eyes, I notice that Hollywood's more toned than I thought he would be, but really pale. He has some pimples on his chest. "Is it okay if I sleep in my boxers?" Hollywood glances at me. "I didn't bring pajamas."

"Fine with me," Ted answers. He's already in his astronaut PJs.

"Don't mind me," I say.

Ted dives for the other bed.

"Hey! That's mine," I protest.

"You can sleep with me," Ted says, winking and raising his eyebrows in an attempt to look sexy. It only succeeds in making me laugh.

"In your dreams, Teddy boy!" I grab a pillow off of each bed. "I'll take the floor." When no one stops me, I throw a blanket down. I don't bother changing out of my clothes.

I can't sleep. Both Ted and Hollywood snore.

I turn on the television. Jackpot! *Nelson's Neighborhood* is on. The dad is so cool. Whenever he goes on business trips, he always brings home exciting presents for the twins and asks how they've been.

I take my father file folder out of my duffel bag and shuffle through the photos. Every mile away from Kissimmee is a mile closer to finding what I'm looking for.

## ★ THIRTEEN ★

**D**espite Ted's incessant begging, we don't do much sightseeing.

"Look! A house made of soda bottles!"

"A museum of broken fenders!"

"A natural geyser!"

Anytime he sees a billboard for a tourist trap, he wants to stop. His AAA guidebook is filled with colorful Post-it notes, and he's keeping a log of every meal we eat. "It's for my autobiography," he explains earnestly.

Hollywood is in a hurry to start his new life. So am I. Going through Texas is hell. The radio won't come in and we have to listen to Ted tell us about his Thai culture, and about how his parents support his independence, and about how he's not really short because he will probably have a growth spurt soon, and about how someday we will all have microchips embedded in us, and about how . . .

"Shut up already," Hollywood barks as he grips the steering wheel.

I look at Ted in the side mirror. He looks hurt, then angry. We drive in painful silence for the next forty-five miles as Ted raises and lowers the window nonstop. Finally Hollywood asks, "Microchips? Don't they already put those in dogs in case they get lost?"

Ted perks right up and begins jabbering again. Hollywood looks at me and mouths, "Sorry."

I smile at him. You can learn a lot about a person on a road trip.

## FOURTEEN

Ted is bopping up and down in the backseat like some sort of deranged baby kangaroo. The sign says that Los Angeles is less than one hundred and fifty miles away.

We are so close.

"So where does Carla live?" Hollywood asks. "Is she expecting you tonight?"

I turn around to face Ted. He's always got everything figured out.

"We thought we'd stay with you for a while," he informs Hollywood.

"What?" Hollywood squawks. "You can't stay with me. I'm in the dorms. I have a roommate. What about Carla?"

"There is no Carla," Ted says. "I made that up so that our parents would let us go to L.A."

"No Carla?" Hollywood sounds mystified. "No Carla?"

"No Carla," Ted says, looking pleased with himself. "So we'll just crash with you until we get our own place."

"No, no, no." Hollywood shakes his head. "I can't have you guys in the dorm. What if we get caught and I get kicked out of school?"

"You won't get caught. It will be fine," Ted assures him. "Trust me."

"Can't we stay, just for a couple days?" I plead. I put on the sad face I've seen Chessy use on her husbands when she wants something. Hollywood looks like he's starting to waver.

"You wouldn't want Maybe on the streets, would you?" Ted asks. "An innocent young thing like that is sure to be taken advantage of."

"I'm the one who's being taken advantage of," Hollywood mutters.

Ted and I glance at each other. We thought he didn't know.

For the next hour, Ted talks to his parents on his cell phone, narrating everything he sees. It's maddening. "Paww, there's a rusted car. . . . There are five birds on the telephone wire. . . . Maybe looks upset. . . . Maybe, Paww wants to know if you're upset."

I'm not upset. I'm . . . I don't know what I am. It's finally starting to hit me that we're really going through with this. I start to panic. What will we do when we get to L.A.? Where will we live? Where will we get money? How will I find my father?

We've passed Palm Springs. Suddenly we all gasp. Two giant dinosaurs loom in the distance. "Paww!" Ted shouts. "I've spotted a brontosaur. . . . No, it's not an optical illusion. . . . It's a place called Cabazon. . . . Cab-a-zon . . . Hollywood's pulling over. Gotta go!"

Hollywood takes out his camera and captures Ted running around the dinosaurs. Then he films me forcing Ted back into the Green Hornet.

We're on the road again. After a while, the traffic slows. "You're listening to KCLA, all hits, all the time!" the DJ shouts.

Ted pulls out a map. "Take the 60 to the 10 West, then exit at the 110 toward downtown. From there, go right to Figueroa."

*HOOOOONK!!!* Even though we are stuck in traffic, the Green Hornet manages to cut someone off. Hollywood looks shaken. I had no idea he could get any paler than he already is. The woman gives us the finger. "You morons!"

Ted yells back at her, "You're beautiful when you're angry." She shakes her head but smiles.

I crane my neck and look out the window. The palm trees seem to go on forever. Painted along the freeway walls are huge murals of kids playing. A billboard for Universal Studios looms over us. Hollywood points to a building in the hills. "That's the Griffith Park Observatory. 'Once you've been up there, you know you've been someplace.' James Dean, *Rebel Without a Cause*."

As traffic lurches forward, I see it first. "You guys . . ."

The Hollywood sign! It looks exactly like it does on television. We all break out cheering.

## ★ FIFTEEN ★

**H**ollywood drags his battered suitcase into the dorm. One of the wheels is missing so it scrapes along the floor. He doesn't seem to notice — he's too busy being thrilled out of his mind.

An Asian girl is sitting behind the reception desk. She's wearing a tattered T-shirt and straw cowboy hat. "*Sawaddee ka,*" Ted says to her. "Greetings! Are you from Thailand?" Anytime Ted sees someone he thinks might be Thai he tries to bond with them.

The girl looks up from her *Psychology Today* magazine and yawns. "Uh, no, I'm from San Francisco. Are you here for the Gifted High School Summer Program? Because if you are, you're in the wrong dorm."

"Why, thank you!" Ted says. "As a matter of fact, my IQ is so incredibly —"

"Excuse me, I'm checking in," Hollywood says, pushing Ted aside.

"Name?" the girl asks.

"Daniel Patrick Jones."

Ted and I snicker. Hollywood never uses his real name. He pretends not to hear us and focuses on the girl. "That's a nice hat," he tells her. "Very stylish."

Oh God, is he trying to flirt? This is so pathetic. Ted and I make faces at each other.

She touches the brim. "Yeah, my *boyfriend* gave it to me," she says, giving Hollywood an I'm-out-of-your-league look. She opens what looks like a recipe box and pulls out an index card. "Daniel, you're on the Cinema Floor. Here's your key. Do you need me to show you to your room?"

"I can find it," Hollywood says, unfazed by the rejection. "I've got my entourage with me. My bodyguard," he motions to Ted. "And my housekeeper."

"That would be me," I say, waving.

The girl doesn't laugh. Instead, she goes back to her magazine. As we head toward the elevator, she calls out, "Daniel?" It takes us a while to realize she's talking to Hollywood. "I almost forgot. There's a message from your roommate. He says he will arrive on Friday."

"Bodyguard?" Ted hisses as we get in the elevator. "Did you not get the memo? I'm with the high-school gifted program."

Hollywood is too happy to bother with Ted. He's finally made it to USC.

The room is small. It barely fits two narrow beds, two dressers, and two desks, each facing opposite walls. There is a window that looks over a parking lot. The closets are tiny. Chessy would never survive here.

"This is so great!" Hollywood shouts. At home, he and his five siblings share bunk beds in a trailer. He does a totally dorky dance around the room. I am so glad I didn't go to the prom with him. It was better for the three of us to hang out at Dairy Queen than to subject the world to Hollywood's attempt at dancing.

"Should we get our stuff?" Ted asks.

Hollywood strokes an imaginary beard. "Here's the deal," he says, picking up his Super 8. "You guys can crash here until Friday when my roommate arrives. Then you have to be out."

Friday. That gives us three days.

"Deal!" Ted says.

"Maybe? Are you okay with that?" Hollywood asks.

"Do I have a choice?"

"Not really."

"Come on, let's explore!" Ted cries as he runs down the hall.

The campus is practically empty. There are lots of trees and old brick buildings. Heritage Hall houses nothing but sports awards. A whole building full of big shiny trophies — Chessy would be so jealous. Next up, Doheny Library. It's massive. I have never seen so many books in my life. I like the smell — sort of sweet and woodsy. They should make a perfume like this. The thick wooden tables and heavy chairs look like they have been here for a hundred years. The stained-glass windows glow. Even the ceiling is beautiful. We are quiet, like we're in church. I wish Ms. Hodor could see this. I could stay here forever, but Ted keeps nudging me toward the door.

The bright sunlight startles me. "Maybe, over here!"

Hollywood is running around on the grass in front of the library. His arms flail and he lifts his knees up high. Ted runs circles around him, literally. For some inexplicable reason, both start hooting. We might as well wear signs that read, WE'RE HICKS FROM KISSIMMEE.

When at last the boys are pooped out, we stop in front of a statue of a soldier. Hollywood stops wheezing long enough to take out his camera. "It's not just any soldier," he says reverently. "It's Tommy Trojan."

"The inventor of the condom?" Ted asks with awe in his voice. "Wow!"

Hollywood films the statue from odd angles. At one point he is lying on the ground shooting up. "Tommy Trojan is a soldier and the symbol of the University of Southern California," he states, like it's something we should know.

"Well, this is boring," Ted announces. "Hey, let's go on a tour of movie-star homes. Hollywood," he coos. "You know you want to. . . ."

## ★ SIXTEEN ★

We keep driving around looking for a cheap parking lot. Apparently, there is no such thing in Los Angeles. The tour bus is idling and ready to go by the time we board. There aren't many people seated. Just us, a pale family from Germany, and a man wearing an orange jumpsuit.

I take a window seat and Hollywood slides in next to me. "The bus is practically empty," I point out. "There's enough room for each of us to have our own row." When he doesn't respond, I shout, "Move!"

Hollywood relocates to the seat behind me. Ted's up front near the driver, peppering him with questions.

"Do the movie stars ever come out and wave at the bus?"

"How do we know Teri Lesesne really lives there?"

"How much do you get paid for doing this?"

"What if you have to go to the bathroom?"

"What if I have to go to the bathroom?"

You'd think the bus driver would smack him, but instead he cheerfully answers all of Ted's questions and even offers him a stick of gum.

As the bus rolls through the hills, Hollywood's busy filming everything, so I just stare out the window and admire the tops of the mansions. They all have walls around them. I wonder what life is like on the other side. Chessy would love this. One time one of her husbands took us to Miami and we drove around the really rich people's neighborhoods.

"Someday," Chessy pledged as we passed a giant pink mansion with a security guard posted in front of it, "we're going to live in a house like that."

After the tour, the bus driver drops us off on Hollywood Boulevard. It's not what I expected. It's a tourist trap. However, if Hollywood is disappointed he hides it well.

At Grauman's Chinese Theatre, there are an alarming number of adults dressed like *Star Wars* characters. Three Chewbaccas are taking pictures of one another. While Hollywood talks to a middle-aged version of Liesl and Friedrich from *The Sound of Music*, I think about my father. I wonder if he's ever been here. Wouldn't it be wonderful if he were here now?

Ted whispers, "Welcome home."

It takes me a moment to get what he means. Then it hits me. Even with my pink hair, white makeup, and black kohl-rimmed eyes, no one is looking at me. In Florida people would stare all the time. Once, when I was at Rite Aid buying a magazine, an old man with an American flag pin in his lapel spit on me. When I complained to the manager, he looked me up and down and then said, "Well, you probably deserved it."

I turn around and spot a girl with bright orange hair. When she notices me, she winks and sticks her tongue out. It's pierced. I clamp my mouth shut.

Ted calls me over and we do the obligatory putting-our-hands-in-the-cement-handprints-of-the-movie-stars, something Chessy has always wanted to do.

"If you're so into movie stars, why don't you just go to Hollywood?" I once asked.

"The train takes forever, you know that," she replied, still keeping her eyes on her celebrity tell-all magazine.

"You could fly."

"Maybelline, you know that the only way I would ever fly is first-class, and that's just way too expensive."

"Oh yeah," I said. "Right. Well, you could take a bus or a train, or drive —"

Chessy's silence told me to shut up. We both knew that the real reason was that her fear of leaving Florida was second only to her fear of cellulite.

My hands are the same size as Judy Garland's. I spy Marilyn Monroe's footprints. Their photos are both on Chessy's Wall of Beauty.

"Okay! I'm officially bored now," Ted bellows. Instantly, all the tourists standing near him move away. Hollywood and I spot each other from across the courtyard and laugh.

At Ted's insistence, Hollywood bids Grauman's farewell and we venture on to the mall next door. There are no malls like this in Kissimmee. This one houses the fanciest bowling alley I have ever seen. A place like this wouldn't even let Jake through the door. If my biological father bowled, this is where he'd be. I check out every middle-aged man in the bowling alley. When one winks at me, I grab Ted and Hollywood and head out.

There are nice stores and a huge movie theater. The restaurants look expensive. We stop in front of the Kodak Theatre. "This is where the Academy Awards take place," Hollywood whispers reverently.

Ted yawns.

We walk up and down Vine Street, taking turns reading the names of the stars on the Walk of Fame. Hollywood feels the need to lecture us about each one in excruciating detail. We would move faster, but Ted seems interested in what Hollywood has to say. He keeps asking him dumb questions, like "Who pays for these?" and "Who do I need to sleep with to get my own star?"

We pass Mickey Rooney's star when suddenly Hollywood comes to a dead stop. Ted and I crash into him. "1719 Vine Street," Hollywood's voice trembles. He takes extra care cleaning the lens before turning on his camera. We all stare at James Dean's star. The silence is broken when Ted spits on it.

"What are you doing?" Hollywood screams, pushing Ted to the ground.

Ted is rubbing his leg. "I was going to spit-polish it," he yells back. "It looked like it needed some cleaning. I was going to do it for you."

Hollywood extends his hand. "Sorry, Ted."

Ted takes his hand. He has to lean on Hollywood as he hobbles to the curb to sit down. I can tell he's faking. Ted will do anything for attention.

Hollywood takes off his T-shirt, polishes the star, and then puts his shirt back on. It's filthy, but he doesn't seem to notice.

Hollywood is so hyped over the star that it takes us four blocks to calm him down. In four blocks the street has changed. There are wig stores, and dollar stores, and lots of liquor stores. The people look grungy. I wonder if they think I do too. This is not the kind of place I would expect to find my father.

We eat dinner at a hot wings joint. Ted takes out his wallet. "Where does the money go?" he asks.

A jolt of panic strikes me. I'm running out of cash and was counting on borrowing money from Ted. What'll we do when our money runs out?

It costs twelve dollars to get the Green Hornet out of the lot. The car's not even worth twelve dollars. It's dark by the time we get back to the dorm. At the front desk an Indian guy listens to classical music as he plays along on his invisible violin. He nods to us as we go upstairs. I want to take a shower, but we don't have any towels or even soap.

Hollywood lies down. There are no sheets or pillows on the bed. That stuff is in the trunk of his car, but Hollywood says, "I'm too tired to go and get it."

Neither Ted nor I volunteer. We're both bushed, but Ted has enough energy left to rush to the other bed before I can get there.

"Fine!" I say. "See if I care."

I use my purse as a pillow. It's lumpy. Before long the guys are snoring. I lay awake and stare at the ceiling.

Okay, so I'm in Los Angeles. Now what?

## ★ SEVENTEEN ★

**H**ollywood's idea of decorating is to stick his USC acceptance letter on his bulletin board. His mother packed linens for him, including a bedspread with basketballs all over it that she picked up at the flea market.

"USC is a football school," Ted tells him.

"USC is a film school," Hollywood replies.

"Football."

"Film."

"Football."

"Film."

Ted reaches over to pat Hollywood on the back. "Poor deluded boy," he tells him. "You have no idea what you're talking about, do you?"

"Film," Hollywood barks.

I leave them to their debate and wander around campus. Some of the students tote around expensive designer handbags and look scary rich. For the most part, though, they look like regular kids, only better looking. One girl, who has a pierced lip and nose, breaks from her group and runs over to me. She hands me a flyer for a Crimefighters concert on the Sunset Strip. "Tell all your friends," she says. "Love your hair! I thought I was the only USC student with hair like that."

I don't tell her that she is.

The days speed by as we explore L.A. We visit the zoo and several museums. Ted's favorite place is the La Brea Tar Pits. Hollywood's roommate is supposed to arrive this afternoon, which means that Ted and I will be homeless.

"How much money do you have?" I ask.

"Not enough," Ted answers. "What about you?"

"Even less."

I wander to the student union to look at the help-wanted board. My heart skips a beat, and even though the sign reads DO NOT REMOVE JOB POSTINGS, I slip one into my purse.

When I return I hear three voices in Hollywood's room. I push the door open and stand frozen as I stare at what has got to be one of the most gorgeous guys on the planet.

"Hello!" he says, standing to greet me. "I'm Ian. You must be one of Daniel's mates."

"Mates?" Ted asks.

"Daniel?" I say.

"That would be me," Hollywood says a little too forcefully.

"But your name is —"

"Daniel," he says, giving me the evil eye.

"Daniel?" Ted snorts. "You're Hollywood."

"I'm Daniel!"

"You're Hollywood!"

"Daniel!"

"Hollywood!"

As Ted and Hollywood shout at each other, I smile and tell Ian, "My name is Maybe."

He extends his hand and we shake. "Nice to meet you, Maybe." His killer British accent is to die for. "Maybe?" he says, looking into my eyes.

"Yes, Ian?" I murmur.

"My hand."

"Oh, sorry!" I say, laughing nervously. I release my grip on him.

Hollywood and Ted are now glaring at each other, but at least they are silent. I attempt to say something witty, but I'm too busy staring at Ian. His rumpled ivory linen suit with a baby blue shirt underneath sets off his creamy dark skin. His face is soft, his features almost delicate. I restrain myself from reaching out to run my fingers through his curly black hair. If this is what college boys are like, I think I may reconsider higher education.

A throat-clearing noise fills the room and breaks the spell. It's Hollywood. "Perhaps Ian wants to get settled," he says.

"You're acting pissy, *Daniel*," Ted replies.

Hollywood's face is blank, but he is blinking rapidly. With his big brown white-person Afro, too-short running shorts, and tattered T-shirt, he looks like the complete opposite of Ian. For the first time, I notice that Hollywood's head seems too small for his body.

Ted is now grilling Ian about the monarchy. "Do you think Princess Diana's death was really an accident? I have a theory . . ."

Hollywood gestures for me to rescue Ian. "Come on, Ted," I say. "Time to clear out." I turn to Ian. "See you later!" I hope I sound carefree and available.

Ian smiles and I melt. "Looking forward to it, then," he says in that to-die-for accent of his.

Ted replies, "Tallyho, mate!"

And we're off.

The minute Ian's out of sight, Ted looks glum, but not me. If I could whistle, I would. "Maybelline," Ted says, stopping in front of Tommy Trojan. "Do you realize what Ian's arrival signals?"

"That I have finally found love?"

"That we're out on the streets."

Geez, leave it to Ted to spoil the moment.

"Well, I have a plan, since it's obvious you don't," Ted informs me.

"What?"

"Dorm lounges. They've got couches, televisions, bathrooms. Students sleep there all the time when they're too hung over or too stoned to find their rooms." I nod. "We can crash lounges until we get enough money for our own place."

"That reminds me. Look!" I wave the job opening in front of Ted.

"Seeking an assistant to a well-known personage in the enter-tainment industry," he reads. His eyes light up. Along with *The New York Times*, *Forbes*, and *Thai World Monthly*, Ted gobbles up all the celebrity magazines. Where Hollywood is interested in film, Ted is interested in fame. He's always telling me, "I am des-tined for great things."

Ted whips out his cell phone. His fingers fly as he dials. "Good afternoon," he says. His voice sounds even deeper than usual. I lean in. He shoves me away and mouths, "Do you mind?"

I walk away and study Tommy Trojan. He's very muscular, like

Ian. Then I head to the library to use the bathroom. There's no toilet paper, so I have to ask the person in the stall next to me to hand me some. She does.

We both come out at the same time. She looks me up and down. It feels like high school. I wash my hands for a long time. When she leaves I glance in the mirror. My eyeliner is all smudged and I have purple lipstick on my teeth. There is a wicked stain on my T-shirt.

This is what Hollywood's to-die-for roommate saw? Why didn't someone tell me? I wash off my makeup and reapply my liner and lipstick. There's nothing I can do for the stain.

As I head back toward Tommy Trojan, Ted comes bounding toward me. "I'm in!"

"You got the job?"

"Nope, I got the interview. Once I do that, I'll have the job. Who wouldn't hire me? What about you? Was there anything for you on the board?"

"Nothing good. I'll probably end up applying at Burger King."

Ted and I kill the rest of the day by checking out all the dorm lounges. We decide it would draw too much attention if we stay in the same one. I decide on Birnkrant Hall — they have a nice couch setup facing the television. Ted selects the international dormitory. He is hoping to run into some students from Thailand and dazzle them with his knowledge of their native culture.

With that settled, all I have left to do is get a job, find a permanent place to live, locate my father, and live happily ever after.

## ★ EIGHTEEN ★

It's one thing to accidentally fall asleep in public, and another to know you are pretending to accidentally fall asleep in public. I wish Ted were here. At night the lounge is pretty empty. The students walking through hardly glance at me. Still, I feel like everyone knows I don't have a place to sleep. Does that classify me as homeless?

## ✯ NINETEEN ✯

**H**ow much?" I ask again. Maybe I've heard wrong.

"Ninety dollars," the pawnbroker says. His arms are totally tattooed.

"But these are nice," I insist. "Real gold and diamonds!"

"This one's fake," he says, holding up the ring from Upton Sinclair. "Listen" — he chews on a toothpick and eyes me — "I'm not asking where you got them, and I'm giving you a good deal. Take it or leave it."

I look at the cluster of Chessy's wedding rings on the counter and let out a sigh. I take one ring back and push the rest toward him. "How much without this one?"

"Sixty-five."

As he counts out the cash in the palm of my hand, I can't help but think, *Sixty-five dollars.* That's the return rate on four of Chessy's six marriages.

I stroll through the University Village, a cluster of stores and food places I can't afford, when I spot a homeless lady pushing a shopping cart. She's wearing a dirty brown coat even though it's boiling outside. Her eyes are wet, like if she were to blink, tears would come pouring out. When she sees me staring, she says, "I have no illusions about my looks. I think my face is funny bunny!"

I give her a weak smile and hurry away.

Back at the dorm, a couple of kids sit on the couch across from me and start to make out. I feel like yelling, "Get a room!" until I realize that's actually *my* goal. So instead, I take refuge in the bathroom.

It smells like cleaning fluid. I suppose it could be worse. After what seems like hours, the kissy couple leaves. It is past midnight. A security guard is roaming around. His shoes make a squeaking sound, like there's water in them. There's a textbook on the floor, science or something, and I bury my nose in it every time he comes near. After he passes I sneak a good look at him. He has an Afro like Hollywood, only his looks normal on him.

On his second pass of the night, he nods at me and I nod back. "My roommate has company," I hear myself explaining, even though he hasn't asked. My voice sounds weird, like it's not mine. "So I prefer to study here. You know, for privacy."

"I didn't know summer school started." The security guard points something at me and I flinch, thinking he's going to shoot. "LifeSaver?" he asks.

Cherry's the next one up. My favorite. "Thank you. I'm getting a jump on my studies." I hold up the book as proof.

"Good for you!" he says before moving on. "I think it's great when kids take the initiative."

That reminds me. I'm supposed to be looking for my father.

## TWENTY

I wake up.

It's 10:30 A.M.

I sit up and rub my eyes. My back hurts. Where am I?

Oh yeah.

My mouth tastes bitter. I remember that my toothbrush is in Hollywood's room. My clothes too, not that I brought a lot of them. I reach for my purse. It's gone. I look under the couch. I dig under the cushions. I race to the bathroom. Maybe I left it there.

It's not there.

I rush to the front desk and clutch the counter. "My purse!" My voice is shrill. "My purse is missing."

The guy's eyes are bloodshot and he has stubble on his face. His elbows are on the desk and he holds his head between his hands like Chessy does when she's hung over.

"My purse is missing," I say, louder this time.

"Let me look in lost and found," he says, standing up in slow motion. "What color is it?"

"Black. Canvas. Black canvas."

He comes back with a pink backpack. "Is this it?"

"No, a black canvas purse. Not a backpack. It has buttons and patches all over it."

He disappears again. "Nothing," he yells from behind a door. He returns and slides a paper across the counter and hands me a pen.

"Fill this out. If we find it we'll call you."

I stare at the form. *Name, dorm, student ID# . . .*

I push it back at him.

"Forget it," I mutter. "Just forget it."

"You're welcome," he says sarcastically. "Have a happy day."

I head to Hollywood's dorm. Ian opens the door. He's only wearing boxers. Plaid. "Pardon me," he says, shutting the door. I stand still, wondering if I should leave. A half second later the door opens again. This time Ian has a robe on. "Sorry about that."

"Is Hollywood here?"

"He's at work."

"My purse got stolen," I blurt out.

"I am so sorry," he says. He really does look sorry. "Is there anything I can do?"

*You could go back to just wearing your boxers,* I want to tell him. Instead, I just shake my head. "Daniel has some of my stuff here, so I thought I'd get it."

He steps aside and lets me in. I gape. Hollywood's side of the room looks the same, with his stupid acceptance letter still tacked on his bulletin board, but Ian's side looks homey. Photos cover his bulletin board, including one of a beauty pageant contestant. His desk is stocked with pens and monogrammed pads of paper. He even has a candy jar set out. He's been here, what? Less than twenty-four hours and already made himself at home.

"Mint?"

I cover my mouth with my hand and try to smell my own breath. "Oh, thanks." I pop the mint into my mouth before my breath can kill him. I point to the photo of the girl. "Nice crown," I say sarcastically.

"That's my girlfriend. The crown's been in her family for generations. Her father is first cousin to a minor royal."

Without knocking, Ted comes bursting through the door. "I GOT THE JOB! Where's Daniel? Congratulate me! You are looking at the new personal assistant to Gloria de la Tour, actress of stage and screen."

"The star of *Find My Way*?" Ian asks. *Find My Way* is a classic. Hollywood tells us that all the time.

Ted nods and does one of those Irish dances where his feet fly but he keeps his hands and arms tightly at his side. Ian looks confused. I grab Ted's arm and yell, "I lost my purse!"

"Gee, Maybe, that's too bad," Ted says, still dancing. "But let's talk about me. I got the job!"

Hollywood doesn't get off of work for a couple hours, so Ted and I bum around as I listen to him talk nonstop about Gloria de la Tour. I visit the bathroom just to get away from him. When I scrub my face, my makeup turns the water gray. I watch it swirl down the drain. I feel naked.

"You look funny," Ted says when I finally emerge.

"So do you. Let's stop at the drugstore. I need some stuff."

I pick up some black eyeliner and find a cheap deep purple lipstick on sale.

"Can I have some money?"

"No."

"Please," I beg. "It won't be that much."

"No. I won't get paid until I've worked a full week."

I go into the next aisle and look around. Nobody's near. I slip the makeup into my pocket.

"Put that back or I'll call the police!"

Startled, I look up. It's only Ted.

"Good one." I laugh nervously.

"I'm serious. I'll turn you in, Maybe."

"Ted, stop joking," I grab his arm and whisper. "Let's get out of here."

He stands firm and glares at me. I glare back, but Ted wears me down. I toss the liner and lipstick at him and storm out.

"I don't know what you're getting so hissy about," he says, running to catch up to me. "You should be thanking me for stopping your crime spree. It's a quick way to land in jail."

I whip around and face him. "I spent the night sleeping in a lounge. I've had my purse and money stolen. My mother's fiancé tried to rape me. I've run away from home. I have no place to live. No job. No nothing. And I came all this way to find a father who doesn't even know I'm alive. How about that for a reason to be hissy?"

Ted mulls this over. "Not bad," he says. "But hurry up and get over your pity party because we have important matters to discuss."

As we sit on a bench facing the cafeteria, Ted launches into another blow-by-blow description of his interview with Gloria de la Tour.

"She was wearing pearls as big as marbles, and when I asked if they were real, she said yes and let me try them on. . . ."

"She said I was very Continental —"

"Excuse me," I interrupt, "but why would a world-famous movie star want to hire you?"

Ted looks miffed. "She was quite impressed with my credentials," he says.

"What credentials? You're a kid from Kissimmee."

"First of all, there's the Youth for a Better Tomorrow Caucus that I founded."

"You're the only member."

"And my letters of reference."

"Those were from your parents."

"No," Ted corrects me, "I had one from Mrs. Escobar, one from Ms. Harper in the attendance office, and one from Congressman Mason."

"How on earth did you wrangle a letter from him?"

"Paww knows someone, who knows someone, whose sister knows him. By the way, Miss de la Tour lives in a mansion, and guess what? I'll be driving her Rolls-Royce!"

I look up. "Say that again?"

"Miss de la Tour lives in a mansion —"

"Not that," I snap. "What exactly will you be driving?"

"Her Rolls-Royce," Ted repeats, puffing his chest out. "When Chauffeur is off, I will be driving the Rolls."

"Let me make sure I understand this. Some old movie star you just met is going to let you drive her Rolls-Royce?"

"Yes!" Ted shouts. "Is this totally cool or is this totally cool?"

"It's absurd."

"I told her that I was an expert driver and that I've even competed on the Grand Prix Raceway in Florida."

"Ted, those were go-karts."

"A car's a car."

I am about to question Gloria de la Tour's sanity when Hollywood shows up in his cafeteria uniform. He's still wearing his hairnet. Hollywood hands me a brown paper bag with my dinner inside. Ted is now recounting his interview for Hollywood. I am far more focused on the cheeseburger and fries. After I finish mine, I start on Hollywood's. He doesn't seem to notice. He's too busy paying attention to Ted, which Ted is lapping up.

"Gloria de la Tour?" Hollywood marvels. "She almost co-starred with James Dean. . . ."

I zone out. I just want to go to bed. I just want a bed.

Afterward, we all head to our respective dorms. As I settle into the couch, the security guard walks past.

"Hi Maybe."

"Hey Parker."

"How's science?"

"Good. How's your daughter?"

Parker stops and takes out his wallet. "She changed her hair," I note.

"Yeah," he says, smiling at the picture. "She wanted to look like Snow White, so my wife cut her hair. Before she cut it, I said, 'Zoey, there aren't any black Snow Whites,' but she didn't care. She just said, 'Well, I'll be the first one.'"

Parker seems like a good dad. I hope mine is too. I wait another half hour even though I'm sleepy. *Nelson's Neighborhood* comes on at one A.M. It's worth the wait. Nelson B. Nelson is conflicted because he accidentally saw the answers to his history test. In the end, his father counsels him about honesty and Nelson confesses to his teacher. She changes the test and he still gets an A. Good ol' Nelson B. Nelson. He has all the luck.

The next morning I wander around and apply for jobs at a couple of places near USC. Since my purse was stolen and I don't have any ID, I'm turned down everywhere I go.

"Without any ID, they might think you're a runaway or something," a nice girl at Gorilla Grill tells me. I pretend to laugh. "Have you told your parents about your purse? Maybe they can send you some money. I always just tell mine I need money for books, and they send it right away."

"Good idea," I say, like that's even a remote possibility.

"Hey, are you hungry?"

"A little." I wonder if she can hear my stomach growling.

"I made too many subs," she says, putting two into a bag. "And we're not allowed to sell them unless they're made fresh and to order."

"Oh, um, well, I don't have my wallet. . . ."

"No charge," she insists. "If you don't take them I'd have to throw them away."

"Thank you. I really mean that."

As I sit on the curb, the homeless lady strolls past me pushing her shopping cart. She sees me eating, licks her lips, and keeps going. I watch her plod along, her bare feet shoved into gray sneakers. "Wait!" I hear myself call out. "Wait up!"

I catch up to her and hold out the unopened sandwich. "I had an extra one," I explain. She narrows one eye at me, like a half squint or maybe a wink. "It's okay, really," I insist.

Her gnarled hands wrap around mine. I tense up. She brings my half-eaten sandwich to her mouth and takes a bite. Her breath is awful. She lets go of my hand and closes her eyes as she chews. When she opens her eyes, they sparkle. "That's good," she murmurs. "Okay, I'll take both. Does it come with melons, or perhaps a nice assortment of cheeses?"

"No, just the sandwich," I answer apologetically.

As she devours her meal, she says in a gravelly voice, "My name's Audrey Hepburn. I live at Tiffany's, that's where I always eat breakfast. Here, I want to pay you for these."

I shake my head. "They didn't cost me anything," I say, slowly backing away.

"I insist," she says, rummaging through her shopping cart. Her hand comes out clutching something. "This is for you." She opens her palm. It's empty. "Good vibes," she says, pleased with herself. "I got lots of them."

"Uh, thanks."

Unfortunately, Audrey Hepburn's good vibes do nothing for me. It's the same story everywhere I go. No one's hiring. At least, no one's hiring *me*.

I end up hanging out in the library. I don't have a library card, but the stacks are big and I can disappear there. Over the past few days I've read Flannery O'Connor and Tom Clancy and even a book claiming World War III is around the corner. But what I've been doing most is looking for my father.

There are banks of computers that sit empty. Most of the students have their own laptops. I type in . . .

Gunnar Los Angeles
Gunnar Hollywood
Gunnar Florida
Gunnar Producer
Gunnar Actor
Gunnar Director

Every Gunnar combination I can think of, I try. Even though I know nothing will come up, I even enter, "Gunnar Chessy Maybelline Family."

If only I had Gunnar's last name. That's when it hits me! My birth certificate. Maybe my father's name will be on it. There are thousands of Internet sites that seem to be set up for the sole purpose of helping me get my birth certificate. For the first time since arriving in Los Angeles, I'm getting somewhere. All I need is:

1) a valid photo ID
2) a credit card
3) to be at least eighteen years old.

Great. I strike out completely.

Next, I Google "birth parents" and three million sites come up. It looks like most are for adoptees. I wish I had been adopted, then I'd have no ties to Chessy. Ted's lucky he doesn't have baggage like I do. Still, it's weird. He has no desire to find his birth parents. He's not even curious.

"Why would I want to find my birth parents?" he said once, looking shocked. "I know who my real parents are. I live with them."

I find a working pay phone and punch in the toll-free number from one of the birth-parent search sites. "Is Gunnar his first or last name?" the lady asks.

"First?"

"I'm so sorry, dear," the lady is telling me. "But with only one name it makes it nearly impossible. Your mother should have the information that should lead you to your father. The best place to start is with her."

I try explaining that she's the last person I want to talk to. It's beginning to dawn on me that without Chessy's help, I'm nowhere.

"There is one thing that we can do," the lady offers. "We can register you in our database. If by chance your father is looking for you, he'd be able to find you here."

I doubt anyone's looking for me, but I give her my information anyway.

With no place else to go, I spend the next couple of days at the library computer contacting other adoption/birth search sites and giving them my information. I use Ted's cell phone number as the way to contact me. It's depressing to think about how many people are looking for someone.

I gather my things and get up to stretch my legs. For fun, I think of a title and look it up in the catalog. I am surprised that it's here. I write down the number and take the elevator to the fourth floor. There it is, among the miles of shelves. *A Little Princess*. I haven't read this in ages. There's an open window on the first floor near the bathroom. Good thing Ted's not here. I toss the book out into the bushes, and then retrieve it.

I spend the rest of the day in Hollywood's room getting lost in the book.

## TWENTY-ONE

**S**ummer school has started. There are more students in the
library now compared to two days ago. There are more students in the dorms too, so Parker's pretty busy. He says that
employees' kids get to go to USC for free; that's why he's working here. Even though Zoey is only seven, he's looking out for
the day she starts college. I wonder if my father went to college.
I'm sure he did. Probably Ivy League.

"What about you, Maybe?" It's three A.M. and Parker's on his
break. He hands me some banana bread. His wife makes the
best banana bread.

"What about me?"

"When did you decide to become a doctor? You're already
keeping doctors' hours, you night owl."

I laugh. "A doctor?"

"You told me you were premed."

"Oh! Right. Premed. Well, I've always really been into the
whole medical thing, helping people. You know."

After Parker leaves, I curl up on the couch. I have about four
hours until students start making their way to breakfast. If I'm

lucky some of them will be in a hurry and leave coffee or bagels on the tables.

Now that Hollywood's obsessed with his screenwriting class and Ted's been working for Miss de la Tour for a few days, they're both happy and excited, caught up in their new worlds. But for me, the days seem to drag on forever.

Hollywood feeds me lunch when he can, but sometimes my only meal is dinner. Ted's in charge of that, although he's been getting off of work later and later. I just wait in Ted's lounge until he shows up. The international students pretty much ignore me. To them, I'm just another foreigner.

One day I find a five-dollar bill on the ground outside the student store. I race over to the drugstore and buy black eyeliner. I wish I had enough for lipstick too.

My stomach is grumbling.

"Uh, Maybe?" Hollywood hands me a greasy paper bag. "This is really hard . . ."

"I know," I tell him, "but isn't it worth it? I mean, look at you. Sure, you're working and going to school, but Hollywood, it's USC! It's your dream come true."

"Yeah, but Maybe, we need to talk. I want to talk about, you know, you being here and stuff."

"Oh. Okay." I bite into the burger. Even though it's cold, it tastes sooooo good. "Listen, Hollywood. You've been great. I'll pay you back for the food when I get some money, I promise."

"It's not just that. All your stuff is still in my room. Ted's things too. And you guys are over all the time. I don't mind, honest. But my roommate —"

"Did Ian say something? I didn't mean to stare that time he came in from the shower. I just, I dunno."

"No, no, it's not that, although that was awkward." Hollywood pauses. "But, well, some of his money is missing and he . . ."

What? "I didn't take it!" I throw my hamburger at Hollywood.

"I never said you did," Hollywood says evenly as he tries to wipe the ketchup off his shirt. "Nor did Ian. If you need money, I can lend you some more."

"Screw you, Hollywood. I didn't take the money."

Hollywood looks miserable. "I'm sorry, Maybe. It's just that I can't have you coming in and out of my room all the time. Our resident advisor said that from now on guests have to sign in, on account of the thefts that have been happening."

I pick up the burger off the ground and chew on it as Hollywood blabbers. I don't even care that he's filming me. "I'll get my stuff out right now," I mutter. "Give me your key."

Ted's at work, catering to glorious Gloria de la Tour's every whim. He's loving his job as much as I am hating my stupid life. Ted can get his own stuff later. On the visitors sign-in sheet I write "Aileen Wuornos." She's Florida's notorious serial killer. The guy just looks at my name and, without bothering to check my ID, says, "Aileen, you can go on up."

The door's unlocked and no one's home. Hollywood was probably the last one to leave. His family never locked their trailers. I grab my duffel bag. There's a twenty-dollar bill on the dresser. I take that too. If Ian thinks I'm stealing from him, I might as well. Finally I swipe all the mints from his stupid candy jar.

As I walk through campus munching on the mints, I look for a place to stash my things. This is really pathetic. I decide on some bushes near Founders Hall. When I part the plants I spy an empty beer can and a yellow sock. Looks like someone's been here before me.

It's starting to get dark. Good. Ted will be back soon.

I wait for him at his dorm. The television is on a Spanish-language station and a bunch of Asian kids are watching. "Anyone mind if I change it to *Nelson's Neighborhood*?" I ask. When no one responds, I sink into the couch and stare at the TV. You don't have to speak Spanish to know that the lady in the red dress is up to no good.

After the lady in red robs a bank and kills two people, Ted shows up. "C'mon, let's grab Hollywood and go for a drive," he shouts as he comes bounding toward me. "We can even invite Ian."

"Ian hates us," I tell him.

"He doesn't hate me. Everyone loves me. I can understand why he hates you, though."

"What's that supposed to mean?"

"Well, just look at you." I thought I looked pretty good, especially since I had just rimmed my eyes with black liner. "You look like you're ready for Halloween. And then all you do is mope around and act like some slug."

"It's not my fault I don't have a cushy job like you," I shoot back.

"Whatever."

Ian claims to be busy, but Hollywood joins us as we head to the parking lot. I am still not speaking to either of them. Ted marches past the Green Hornet.

"Hey, where are you going?" Hollywood calls out.

Ted just smiles. We turn the corner and all freak out at once.

"Get in," Ted says, opening the door to the Rolls-Royce.

"Hot damn!" Hollywood shouts.

"Ohmygod!" I scream and slide across the smooth leather seats. "Ohmygod!"

Ted starts the car and inches out of the parking space. It doesn't even sound like the engine is on. We drive down Rodeo Drive in Beverly Hills. Tourists try to look into the car to see if we are somebodies.

"Chauffeur is on vacation, so Miss de la Tour says I am her driver for the week," Ted boasts.

Hollywood runs his hand over the shiny wooden dashboard. "Does she know you have the car now?"

Ted doesn't answer. He's too busy turning the windshield wipers on and off. "The engine is handmade," he finally says. "Guess how much this car costs. Just guess."

"Forty thousand dollars?" I throw out. I've never been that into cars. I haven't even taken driver's training yet. Chessy refused to let me get my license. "Why do you need to drive?" she asked. "You never go anywhere."

"One hundred thousand dollars?" Hollywood ventures.

"Over a quarter million dollars!" Ted screams. He swerves sharply to the left to miss hitting a pole. Ted can barely reach the pedals, so he scoots up and down in the driver's seat — down to press the gas or brakes, up to see over the steering wheel.

Hollywood whistles. "We bought our double-wide trailer for twenty-four thousand five hundred dollars. It was used."

We are driving down Melrose Avenue now. It seems crowded for a Thursday night.

"Pull over," I shout. "There's a parking spot!"

"Why . . ." Ted starts to ask.

"Just do what I tell you!"

Ted does a dismal job at parallel parking.

I turn to Hollywood. "Hand me your wallet."

"Why?"

"Just do it," I order. "Stay in the car; I'll be right back."

Fifteen minutes later, I return. I toss Hollywood's wallet to him and hand Ted a bag. Cautiously, he opens it. "What are these for?"

"For you. So you can reach the pedals and drive. They had tons of them in the retro store."

"I'm not wearing these!"

"No one can see your feet when you drive. Put them on."

Hollywood films Ted slipping on the platform shoes and wobbling around the sidewalk. He looks like a baby duck, or a baby lamb, or some baby something learning how to walk.

Finally, we all get back into the car and Ted starts the engine. Slowly he maneuvers the car out of the spot. He has a contented smile on his face, which gets wider the farther we drive.

"Well?" I ask.

"A-list!" he replies.

Ted pulls up to a nice restaurant on Beverly Boulevard. The valet guys race to open the doors for us. Ted tips all of them. I notice he doesn't change his shoes.

"What are we doing here?" I whisper. "This place looks expensive."

Hollywood keeps his camera rolling.

"I'm taking my friends out. Today was payday," he announces.

"I don't have a problem with this," Hollywood says.

"Order anything you'd like," Ted tells him.

Ted sits on one side of the booth and Hollywood and I take the other side. It is so cushy and comfortable, I could live here. Hollywood sits a little too close to me.

"Do you mind?" I say.

He turns red. "Sorry."

Ted pats the seat next to him. "Here, you can sit next to me and give Miss Grumpy her space."

Reluctantly, Hollywood sits next to Ted. "Thank you," I say to both, and then make a big deal about stretching out.

After the calamari appetizer, which Hollywood refuses to eat, Ted clears his throat. "I have an announcement to make. Miss de la Tour has invited me to live with her. She says I can live in the guest apartment above the garage."

"Oh my God, this is so great." I reach across the table to grab Ted's hand and give it a squeeze. "We finally have our own place."

Before he can answer, the unmistakable sound of Ted's cell phone blasts. "Hello? Paww! I'm here with Hollywood and Maybe. Oh yeah. And Carla too. Carla, say hello to my father."

I shake my head when Ted puts the phone in my face. Hollywood leans in and in a really high voice says, "Hi, Mr. Schneider."

I burst out laughing and have to cover my mouth. For the first time in a long time I feel happy. I am so relieved that we finally have a decent place to live. This is a night for celebrating.

"Love you too, Paww!" Ted says. "Good-bye." He's usually really happy after he talks to his parents, but he looks worried.

"Is everything okay?" I ask.

"Maybe, there's something I need to tell you," Ted says.

Hollywood's eyes dart back and forth between the two of us. He picks up his camera.

"What?" I ask. My good mood starts fading fast.

Ted refuses to meet my gaze. "Miss de la Tour says I am not allowed to have overnight guests. She's very security conscious."

"I've heard that about her." Hollywood nods in agreement. "Ever since that stalker tried to attack her after she won her second Oscar, Gloria de la Tour doesn't trust anyone."

I am still processing Ted's announcement. Hollywood will be living in his dorm room. Ted will be living on some old movie star's estate. And I will be living where?

Oh wait, that's right. In a lounge.

"This is screwed," I say as I push Hollywood's camera away.

"What do you want me to do?" Ted protests. "Tell Miss de la Tour I'd rather stay illegally in the dorms than have my own place? By the way," he adds, "Cook will prepare my meals."

"You're my idol!" Hollywood cries.

Ted holds up his hand and they high-five.

As the two of them discuss how amazing Ted's life is, I start to panic. It's too late to go home, not that I'd want to. I can't, anyway. I have no money. No place to live. Hollywood's sick of me, and now with Ted being sucked into the mysterious world of Gloria de la Tour, I'm going to be totally on my own.

If only I could find my father. He'd take me in.

## ⋆ TWENTY-TWO ⋆

**M**aybe, you can't stay here."

"Huh?" Someone is gently shaking my shoulder. I wipe the sleep from my eyes. "Dad?"

"Maybe, can I see your student ID?"

It's Parker. His usual smile is absent.

"I . . . I lost it."

"We got orders to be really vigilant about loiterers and, well, Maybe, I know you don't live in the dorms."

I'm awake now.

Parker hands me a loaf of banana bread, then opens his wallet. Instead of showing me a photo of his daughter, he gives me eighty dollars.

"A loan," he says when I start to protest. "It's just a loan, Maybe. It doesn't mean anything. Listen, I didn't see you tonight, but tomorrow, you can't be here. Do you understand? I could get fired. I'm sorry."

I nod and take the money.

"Thanks, Parker."

## ★ TWENTY-THREE ★

I've been sleeping in the Green Hornet for the last few days. Ted's been so busy with Miss Onerous Old-Time Movie Star that I hardly see him. All I do all day is hang out at the library. My latest quest is looking up all the television shows and movies that were produced the year I was born. Then I try to see if any were shot in Florida. I keep hitting dead ends. It's frustrating.

There are some real students waiting their turn for the computers. I give mine up and head out to lunch. I've got Parker's money in my pocket but save it. You'd be surprised by the quality of food you can find in the trash. My technique is to watch people eating, then, when they're done, follow. As soon as they dump their food in the trash and leave, I swoop in. I've found that when I target really skinny girls, I can practically get a full meal.

As I'm eating what's left of someone's roast beef sandwich, I spot Hollywood's roommate. I try to run away before Ian sees me, but it's too late.

"Hello Maybelline! I haven't seen you in ages. How are you?"

"Fine."

"How are your classes?"

"Fine."

"Did you hear, they found the guy who was stealing from the dorms? It was an engineering student. He's going to be expelled."

"Really? That's nice. I'd love to stay and chat, but I'm late for class."

"Oh! What are you taking?" Ian asks as I turn away.

"Nuclear physics!" I yell as I hurry off with nowhere to go.

I keep running until I get to University Village. Suddenly, I think about Parker's money. I had resolved to only use it for emergencies, but then it hits me. Of course. If anything ever constituted an emergency, this would be it.

I go to the store for supplies, then head to Burger King. It's three o'clock in the afternoon, so it's not too crowded. I order a large Dr. Pepper and keep the cup when I'm done.

There's no one in the bathroom. I set my duffel bag on the floor and line up everything on the metal shelf above the sink: a small bottle of conditioner, Saran Wrap, rubber gloves, and two packets of Jamaica Kool-Aid. It's a new flavor and the fake fruit on the package is bright, bright red. Beautiful. Chessy always said that a trip to the beauty shop can turn your life around.

Before I begin, I take out a pair of scissors and start chopping away, slowly at first, then faster and faster. When did my hair get this long? As I am cutting, there's a knock on the door. A kid in a Burger King outfit carrying a bucket and a mop comes in. He takes one look at me, blushes, and stammers, "I'll come back later."

Finally I put the scissors down and tear open the Kool-Aid packets, checking again to make sure they are the unsweetened kind. Once I used presweetened and my hair turned into a giant wad of chewed gum. I pour the Kool-Aid into the empty soda cup and add some conditioner, but not too much. Then I stir it all with a couple of straws until it's goopy. I slip on the rubber gloves.

As I am rubbing my homemade concoction into my hair, the bathroom kid comes in again and stares at me.

"What?" I ask, glaring at him.

He mutters something and disappears again.

After I've emptied the soda cup, I wrap my head in Saran Wrap and wait. And wait. And wait.

The door opens. This time it's an older guy. He's alone. His Burger King uniform looks too small, like the buttons are going to pop.

"Miss," he says sternly, "we are going to have to ask you to leave."

I wonder who "we" are. "But I need twenty more minutes," I try to explain. "And then I have to rinse and condition."

"We are going to have to ask you to leave," he repeats firmly. I can tell he is getting off on bossing me around.

"You're just jealous because you don't have any hair," I say.

"Young lady, get out. Now!"

He stands there and watches me gather my things, then escorts me out. I glare at the Burger King flunkie, who pretends not to notice me.

Outside, I sit on the curb. Audrey Hepburn sits down next to me. I scoot over. "I don't bite," she says, "unless it's called for."

Her cart is full of old clothes and paper bags and shiny discs that looks like garbage, but if you look closely you can see they're flattened soda cans. The battered teddy bear tied to the handle of the cart is missing one eye.

"Nobody wants Madonna to be president," Audrey Hepburn says too loudly. Her face is dirty. She's not wearing her coat today, but she still has snow boots on. "They asked me, but I was busy saving the world. What they should do is make cars fly, that way the freeways won't be so crowded. People think that I know everything. I once was so hungry I ate a toothpaste pie."

I keep my eyes fixed on the traffic light. Red. Green. Yellow. Red. Audrey Hepburn inches closer to me and I inch away from her. I want to get up and run away, but that would be rude.

"I like your hat," she says. "What kind of reception do you get? Sometimes I wear tinfoil."

I absentmindedly touch the Saran Wrap on my head.

"What's that black around your eyes? Does it help you see better? I like cake. Guess how much I weighed when I was born."

Audrey Hepburn reminds me of someone. But who?

Oh God. I just figured it out.

The crazy lady sounds like Ted and looks like me.

## ★ TWENTY-FOUR ★

**N**ew hair?" Hollywood asks. I nod. "It looks bright."

The longer you leave the Kool-Aid mix on your head, the brighter it gets. The brighter it gets, the longer it will last. This should last a lifetime.

Ted has the night off. Some ancient Italian prince is squiring Miss de la Tour around town. We're in the Rolls. I'm in the front, Hollywood's in the back.

"Here," I say to Hollywood. I hold out twenty dollars from Parker's money. "I'll pay you the rest I owe you later."

Instead of taking it, he hands me money.

"What's this for?"

"The bus."

"Why would I need bus money?"

"To get home."

Ted fills up the dead air by continuing a conversation that never was. " . . . so I got more platform shoes. It's my signature look. Miss de la Tour thinks I am very stylish . . .

"Miss de la Tour says I am the only person she's ever had working for her who can organize her social calendar . . .

"Miss de la Tour says I look good in warm colors . . .

"Miss de la Tour says I am the son she never had . . .

"Miss de la Tour says —"

"SHUT UP!" I yell. "I am sick of Miss de la Turd!"

Ted glares at me, then clutches the steering wheel and cranes his neck forward like an old person.

I turn around and face Hollywood, who's sitting in the backseat staring out the window. "Are you trying to get rid of me?" I ask softly.

Without looking at me, he says, "Maybe, it's just that I don't think things turned out the way you thought they would."

"You mean, you don't think things turned out the way *you* thought they would."

"What's that supposed to mean?"

I shake my head. "Ted, talk some sense into him. He thinks I should go back to Kissimmee."

"I'm not talking to you," Ted growls. "You're mean. And if I were talking to you, I'd have to agree with Hollywood."

"I can't believe you guys are ganging up on me like this! I thought you were supposed to be my friends."

"We are your friends," Hollywood says. He turns on his camera and shines the light in my face.

"Shut that stupid thing off. Stop the car. Stop the car!"

Ted puts the blinker on and slowly maneuvers to the curb. I grab the door handle and push hard. "You guys are full of it!"

"Good riddance, Maybelline!" Ted shouts. "Hollywood and I will be much happier without you!"

As I storm down the street, Ted follows in the Rolls.

"Get in, Maybe." He lowers his voice. "This is not the best area."

I keep marching ahead, refusing to look at him.

"Get in," he orders, his voice getting deeper so that it sounds like a bullhorn.

There's a group of men on the corner. They're drinking out of paper sacks. The one with the beard looks at me and starts hooting, "Hey, baby, how much?"

I try to ignore him but can't when he blocks the sidewalk. I step back, then jump into the Rolls. As Ted speeds away, I hear the man shout, "We would have paid you double!" The rest of them break out laughing.

We go a couple miles in silence, until Ted says, "There is one other alternative. I think I know of a place where you can live."

"I'm not going to a homeless shelter or some youth detention place," I grumble. I hold my hand out to block the light from Hollywood's camera.

"It's nothing like that," Ted assures me. "In fact, if I'm figuring this right, it's probably very nice."

Suddenly I am too tired to argue. "Whatever. I really don't care anymore. Just as long as I don't have to go back to Kissimmee. Don't make me go back there. Ted," I plead, "don't make me go back."

## ★ TWENTY-FIVE ★

I take a shower in the gym. There's a person who checks IDs, but if it's busy and you act like you belong, they don't bother. I wish I had known this earlier.

Ted's got errands to run before he takes me to this secret location. I am beginning to suspect that he got us a place of our own. I heard him tell his mother that he was moving out of Carla's apartment. Just the thought of it leaves me giddy.

I still have Hollywood's money. Maybe I can get a fake ID so I can get a job. In the meantime, I am at Suds. I like the mini boxes of detergent in the vending machine. They look cute, like doll accessories. I choose a red one that says OXYGEN ACTION on it.

Before my mother married the banker, and she insisted on a washer and dryer for a wedding gift, we had to go to the laundromat. Chessy would buy me a Snickers and then settle in with her movie magazines. I'd sit nibbling on my candy bar and watch the laundry go 'round and 'round.

One time I wandered off and a man with a gold tooth grabbed me and began whispering nasty things in my ear. His breath smelled like an alley. I screamed and Chessy came running. She chased the man away, then held me tight.

That was a long time ago.

It feels good to watch the clothes in the washer. I buy a Snickers from the vending machine. It eats my change, but I don't let that bother me. I'm not going back to Kissimmee and that makes me happy.

Ted won't tell me anything about our new place. I think he wants to surprise me. When he finally shows up, he's all smiles. I am too. I'm not Audrey Hepburn with a shopping cart. I have friends, and soon I will have a place to live.

"I told you not to eat so much fried food . . ." Ted is talking to his mom on the phone as he changes lanes. He's become really good at driving the Rolls. "Hot water. You should drink hot water. Does Paww know you're not feeling well? No, well then, tell him. Yes, tell him. Do you want me to tell him —"

I roll down the window and let the breeze wash across my face as I watch the palm trees parade past us. The Hollywood sign is in the distance. Ted's off the phone now and chattering about Gloria de la Tour. I just smile and listen.

"Miss de la Tour's housekeeper thinks I'm really smart . . ."

"Miss de la Tour keeps her Oscars in a glass case . . ."

"Miss de la Tour was married almost as many times as your mother . . ."

Ted speeds up as we get on the freeway. He keeps driving and doesn't exit at Beverly Hills, where Gloria de la Tour lives.

"Did she kick you out, or did you opt out of the garage apartment?"

"What are you talking about?"

"Our place. We're going to our place, aren't we?" I say smugly. "Listen, Ted, I'm no dummy. I figured it out!"

When Ted remains silent, my voice rises. "You said you knew where I could live. I assumed . . ."

"Maybe, I'm staying with Miss de la Tour. I'm moving out of the garage apartment and into the main house. I'll have my own room and bathroom and the run of the place, plus I'll be right there if Miss de la Tour needs me. You will be living elsewhere."

"Elsewhere?"

Where the hell is elsewhere? Is Ted taking me to the bus station? I will not go back! When he refuses to answer, I don't ask again. I don't want to know. It's better not knowing.

I hate Ted.

Suddenly, the freeway ends. If this is the end of civilization, it looks nice. As we drive up the coast I take in the sun and the sand. Beautiful people in bathing suits cavort in the water. Construction sites vie for space along the strip of land that leans up against the beach. The farther we go, the fancier the homes get. Finally we turn on a side street that winds up the hills. Ted stops the car in front of a house that looks like it's made of glass.

"Where are we?"

"Your new home," he says as he sets the emergency brake. "For now."

I am so confused. Wait! Did Ted find my father? I'll bet he's found my father. What if he found my father? It makes sense he would live in a fancy house like this.

I love Ted.

My heart is racing.

I follow Ted to the front door. He rings the bell. After a long wait, a young woman answers. She scowls down at Ted. "Yes?"

Then she fixes her eyes on me and squints for the longest time before saying, "Oh. It's you. Is your mother with you?"

I shake my head. This is beyond weird. My knees are weak. I reach out to lean against the door so I don't fall over. I wish I was wearing nice clothes.

"May we come in?" Ted asks, already stepping forward.

"If you have to," the young woman says, moving aside. She looks like a model. A mean model.

From the entryway I can see the ocean. This is like one of those houses in a magazine. Suddenly I gasp. I cannot believe what I am seeing.

The walls are covered with photos of Chessy.

There are even some of me.

"It was only a matter of time before one of you showed up." Miss Model lights up a really skinny cigarette. "Make yourselves at home." She looks me up and down and doesn't even try to hide her disgust. "He should be back soon. I'm sure you'll want to catch up."

## ⋆ TWENTY-SIX ⋆

It's been over an hour of awkwardness. Nothing like this ever happened on *Nelson's Neighborhood*. As Ted keeps up a monologue about how his father was twice voted Osceola Rodeo Clown of the Year, Miss Model chain-smokes and never takes her eyes off of me. My freak-out factor is so intense I'm not sure if I am even breathing.

At last, the front door opens. I brace myself.

A voice calls out, "Willow, who owns that Rolls-Royce parked in front of the house?"

The man freezes when he sees me. I do the same. Then he opens his arms and I fly into them. He hugs me tight. It feels so good, I never want to let go.

"Maybe?" he says. "Is it really you?"

"Sammy? Oh my God, it's you!"

"Oh geez," Miss Model says, rolling her eyes.

"Is your mother here?" Sammy asks, eagerly looking around.

"Just me," I say apologetically. "Just me and Ted — that's my friend Ted over there."

Ted puts down the sculpture he was examining and strides over to shake Sammy's hand. "Nice digs you got here, Sam."

Sammy doesn't know Ted, although Ted knows everything about Sammy. He's heard me talk about him a lot. Sammy gives me another hug. He smells the same, like coffee and trees. "Maybe, it's great to see you! Let me look at you. Wow, you've grown up. What are you doing in California?" He turns to Miss Model. "Get these kids something to eat, will you?"

She snuffs out her cigarette and huffs out of the room.

"Your wife?" I ask.

"Girlfriend. But you! Let's talk about you! Maybe, you look so different."

I touch my newly Kool-Aided hair. "I know," I say apologetically. Suddenly I wish my hair was plain and long, and that my eyes weren't rimmed with kohl and my lips weren't purple.

"My Little Maybe isn't so little anymore. Look at you, you're almost as tall as me!"

I start to cry. Sammy always called me his Little Maybe. After Chessy divorced him the second time, I felt an emptiness that was only filled when I met Ted.

When Sammy passes Ted a box of tissues to give to me, Ted starts sobbing and making honking sounds. Then he hogs the tissues as I tell Sammy my story. I leave out the part about looking for my biological father. Somehow, I think that might make him feel funny. It makes me feel funny. And I skip the part about Jake trying to rape me. It's not something I want to discuss. Instead, I say that Chessy and I had a huge fight, which is true.

Because he asks, I tell Sammy about Chessy and the husbands she's had since him, only I try to make it sound like they didn't mean anything to her. Partly because I know that's what he wants to hear, and partly because I know that it's true. She cried over Sammy. He was the only one she really cared for. Still, she didn't care enough to get on a plane and fly to California. Instead, she drank herself into a deep depression that neither of us has recovered from yet.

There's a big crash in the next room. Sammy and I look up. When did it get dark? Miss Model never did come back.

"Sam," Ted says, strolling out of the kitchen and flipping on the lights. He's munching on a huge sandwich. "Sorry about that jar of pickles. Hey, Sam, can Maybe stay with you for a while? She's homeless. I'd let her stay at my mansion, but my old lady has rules."

"Are you homeless?" Sammy asks, surprised.

"Noooo," I say slowly. "I just don't have any place to stay at the moment."

"Of course you can stay here," Sammy says. "I insist."

Ted winks at me. It's not such a bad option, actually. For the first time in California, something feels right. "Well, maybe just for a couple days, if it's no trouble . . ."

"Maybe," Sammy says, "of course it's no trouble. If you didn't stay here, I'd just worry about you. Do you remember how much I used to worry about you?"

I nod. One time when I was little, Chessy passed out and I wandered away. Hours later, Sammy found me. I had fallen asleep under the kiddie slide at the park. I will never forget the look of relief that crossed his face when he woke me up and carried me home.

I try not to start crying again.

"There's just one thing," Sammy is telling me. "You have to call your mother and let her know where you are and who you're with."

"I can't do that," I protest.

"Maybe's run away from home. She's supposedly living with Carla," Ted explains. "Do you have any chips? Barbeque would be great, and dip. Did someone say 'onion dip'?"

"Who's Carla?" Sammy asks.

Ted shrugs. "Hell if I know."

As Ted searches for chips and dip, Sammy plops down on the couch and rubs his forehead. He looks the same as when he lived with us. Same Levi's and crisp white collared shirt. Same open face, same boyish looks. His hair is longer than before, almost touching his shoulders. He always did look handsome, like a surfer all grown up. I remember wishing I looked at least a little bit Chinese, so people would think he was my real dad.

Ted returns with more sandwiches, regular chips, and a pitcher of lemonade. He sets them down on the wood coffee table. There is a flower in a vase on the tray. I tune back in to hear Sammy still talking. ". . . and then if your mother says it's okay, then it's okay with me."

Wordlessly, Ted flips open his cell phone and offers it to me. I hesitate and for a moment everything stops. Finally I take the phone from Ted and dial. It rings and rings until the answering machine picks up. Chessy hasn't bothered to change the message and I hear my old Florida self say, "No one's home. Leave a message."

"Uh, Chessy, it's me," I start to say. Sammy and Ted nod encouragingly. "It's Maybe. Your daughter. I'm in California with Ted and Hollywood. I'm staying with Sammy. Sammy Wing, your second and fourth husband. That's all." I hang up.

Sammy takes the phone from my hand and hits redial. "Hey Chess, Sammy here. Hope you're doing well. Maybe's with me. Everything's fine. Call me, okay?" He leaves his number.

Ted looks at his Mickey Mouse watch. "This has been fun, but I gotta go. Maybe, I'll see you tomorrow. Sam, keep in touch. Here's my number in case our girl causes you any problems."

"Wait, my bag's in the car!"

As we walk to the Rolls, I ask Ted, "Why didn't you tell me you were taking me to Sammy?"

"You would have just complained or refused to go."

He knows me pretty well.

"How did you find him?" I ask.

"It wasn't hard. I knew he lived in California. I knew he was a photographer. And I knew his name. So I just looked him up."

If only finding my biological father could be that easy.

Sammy is still standing in the same spot when I return with my duffel bag. He has a wide grin on his face. "Maybe," he says, hugging me again.

I hug him back. When we finally let go, he asks, "Who was that kid?"

"Thammasat Tantipinichwong Schneider. Also known as Ted, or my best friend."

"Interesting person," Sammy notes. "He wears platform shoes?" I nod. "Was that Rolls-Royce his?"

"That's his boss's car. He works for Gloria de la Tour."

"The movie star?"

"Yep."

"The elusive Miss Gloria de la Tour," he muses. "I thought she was dead."

I gesture to the walls covered with portraits of Chessy. "Uh, Sammy? What's with this?" In some photos she's posing, looking every inch the beauty queen she once was. But the most beautiful shots are the candids, like the one of her hugging a happy little girl with pigtails and missing teeth.

"What can I say?" Sammy gives me a sheepish smile. "Some people drink, some smoke, some do drugs. I took photos of your mom." He pauses, then adds, "I'm over that now."

"Yeah, it would be hard to take her photograph from three thousand miles away!" Sammy laughs, but I can see a flash of sorrow on his face. Quickly, I say, "Nice place here!"

"I'm doing okay." Sammy has always been modest. "I shoot a lot of editorials for magazines, and I'm still doing portraits. Should we eat?" he asks, pointing to the sandwiches.

Suddenly I realize I'm starving. I devour my turkey sandwich while Sammy watches. When I am done, he hands me his and I eat that too. He doesn't criticize me for eating too much.

"Are you sure it's okay that I'm here?"

"Willow will pitch a fit, but it's my house."

"She's pretty."

"So are you," Sammy says. "Come on, I'll show you to your room."

It makes me smile when I see that he still wears cowboy boots.

There are three levels in the house. I assume his room is upstairs. We go downstairs. Lining the walls are framed magazines. Many feature celebrities. I recognize some of the covers. "Did you shoot these?"

Sammy nods. When he pushes open the door to the guest room, I drop my duffel bag. It hits the floor with a loud thud.

There is an awkward silence.

Sammy clears his throat. "Uh, well, I'll give you some privacy so you can unpack. I'll put fresh towels in the bathroom. Help yourself to anything in the kitchen. If I knew you were coming I would have stocked the kitchen with mint Oreos. Are they still your favorite?" I nod. "Consider this your home, Maybe. Get some rest. We'll talk tomorrow."

All I can do is stare at the room. I hear Sammy coming back. I whip around to face him. I have so many questions. But it's not Sammy, it's Willow.

"It's freakin' weird, isn't it?" she mutters, then takes a long drag on her cigarette. She exhales slowly, right in my face.

As the smoke whirls around my head, I nod. It is freakin' weird.

The room is bathed in pink. There's a canopy bed with a white lace bedspread and purple heart-shaped pillows. The wicker rocking chair in the corner is filled with dolls and stuffed animals. A poster of Nelson B. Nelson from *Nelson's Neighborhood* is on the wall. In a silver frame on the dresser is a black-and-white photo of Sammy, my mother, and me taken on the day of their second wedding.

It's a dream bedroom — for a ten-year-old girl.

I wonder what my life would have been like if I grew up in this room, overlooking the ocean, instead of above a charm school in Kissimmee.

"I've got some of my stuff in here," Willow says, brushing past me. Her voice is high-pitched and slightly nasal. "But you can just move it anywhere. After all, it's your room. It always has been."

Before I can thank her, she's gone.

I unpack my stuff. It doesn't take me long. Some of the drawers are full of mini shampoo bottles and pieces of ribbon and other things you wouldn't think you'd find in an expensive house like this. Finally I come across an empty drawer and put my clothes in it. There are wooden hangers in the closet, but I have nothing worthy enough to be hung up.

I sit on the bed, then get up immediately like it's on fire. I don't want to get the bedspread dirty. From the window is a view of the ocean. A full moon reflects on the water and lights up the sky.

I am on overload. Snippets of memories race forward, then fade away. I rub my temples and try to recall when I was ten. Sammy had already bought the house, this house, and our plane tickets. He gave me a red duffel bag to put my most precious belongings in — the same bag I have with me today. Chessy insisted to Sammy, "Go ahead, hon, you get things set up. Maybelline and I will pack up the apartment and close the charm school. Then we'll join you."

We never did make it. Well, one of us didn't, anyway.

As I head to the bathroom, I hear Willow and Sammy upstairs.

"She's *what*???"

"She's staying here until she gets her life sorted out."

"Oh great. And how long will that be? One day? Two? A week? A month? Forever?"

"I don't know."

"You don't know. You don't know? How could you do this without asking me?"

"I didn't know I needed your permission. It's my house. Willow, she's my daughter."

"Your *ex*-stepdaughter. This is about the mother, isn't it? You've never gotten over her. Look! Look around, you've got her photos everywhere. . . ."

I go into the bathroom and shut the door. Even here, on the

other side of the country, I can't get away from Chessy. I scrub my face until it's red and raw. Then I head to bed, but first I open the window. The smell of the salt air surprises me, and I breathe deeply, greedily, trying to inhale as much as I can, before sinking down into the soft mattress. At last, somewhere between the sounds of Sammy and Willow arguing, and the ocean lapping the shore, I begin to drift off to sleep.

I am ten years old. Safe in my bedroom in Kissimmee. I am deliriously happy because soon I will be moving with my mother and stepfather to a new house in a new place, all our own. Even though they have been fighting a lot, I know that once we get to California, everything will be all right.

## ★ TWENTY-SEVEN ★

**S**ammy may be really nice, and have a trendy house, and be all artsy with his photos, but he's still an adult. Over breakfast he lectures me as Miss Model stabs at her grapefruit half with a spoon. It's as if the cool I-want-to-help-you Sammy has morphed into the parental-unit let's-be-sensible Sammy.

"I spoke to your mother this morning," he says as he pours himself a second cup of coffee. I recognize the mug. It's the one with Snoopy dancing that I gave him on our last Christmas together. "She said you can stay."

"Did she say anything else?" I take a bite of my French toast and try to act casual.

"That's it." He sounds apologetic. "How old are you now, fifteen?"

"Sixteen, almost seventeen."

"Well, you can't just hang out all summer. So I expect you to go out and try to get some work, or sign up for summer school, or whatever kids your age do."

*They fight off rapists, watch their mothers turn on them, and run away,* I'm tempted to say. But instead I put on a smile. "Sounds like a plan!"

I can't afford to get Sammy mad at me. He might send me home.

Sammy leaves for work. He's shooting a portrait of a family on their Santa Barbara estate and won't be home until late. Willow and I sit at the far ends of the table and try to ignore each other.

Something about her is familiar. I sneak glances as she scans the newspaper, circling fashion ads and drawing mustaches and tails on the models. Willow's really skinny and tall, like supermodel tall, but she slouches. She looks a lot younger than Sammy. Her skin is translucent and her breasts are fake. Some mothers teach their daughters things like "Look both ways before you cross the street." My mother taught me that "Big breasts on a thin girl are always bought and paid for."

Suddenly, I realize who Willow reminds me of. Blonde hair, upturned nose, big boobs . . .

I'm no longer hungry. I get up and take my dishes with me. As I pass, Willow turns the page and mutters, "Great, the Santa Anas are coming again."

"The Santa Anas?"

"I hate the Santa Anas and so does Sammy, but they're coming and there's nothing we can do to stop them."

"That's too bad," I say, even though I still have no idea who they are. Maybe they're clients of Sammy's. I wonder if my being here will get in the way. I resolve to stay in my room anytime Sammy or Willow has company.

"I'm outta here," Willow announces. She has an audition for a television commercial, something about "a breath mint so minty, it takes your breath away!"

I stare at the huge black-and-white photo on the dining room wall. Chessy is caught off guard with a towel wrapped around her head. She's wearing her bathrobe and nothing else, not even makeup. She would die if she ever saw it, but I think that she never looked better.

I clear Willow's dishes and start up the dishwasher. Then I sweep the kitchen. I pick up the newspaper off the floor and stare up the stairs. Since Sammy and Willow are both gone, I figure it's safe. Still, I tiptoe.

There are two bedrooms and two more bathrooms. One bedroom has been turned into an office. Sammy's telescope sits in the corner. I remember it from when he lived with us. We were always going to the roof to see the stars, Sammy and me. I peer through the eyepiece, but the lens is cracked and dirty and everything is out of focus. It looks like it hasn't been used in a while.

On the desk is a computer, stacks of papers, and a photo of Chessy. There's a photo of me on the wall. It's the one I've always liked. The one where I look happy.

The second bedroom is the biggest one in the house. The bed is huge and covered with a thatched canopy, so it resembles something you'd see on a tropical island. The ceiling fan is made of what looks like bamboo and banana leaves. The master bathroom has a sunken-in tub that looks out over the ocean. There's a walk-in closet that's bigger than my room at home. Most of it is filled with Willow's clothes. One entire wall is lined with shoes.

On one nightstand is a *Catwalk* magazine. Perfumed candles fight for space with an ashtray full of cigarette butts. On the other nightstand is a biography of Diane Arbus, an alarm clock, and a framed photo. In it, Sammy's sporting a tux, Chessy's dressed in a white wedding gown, and I'm in a pink flower-girl dress and cradling a huge bouquet. We are all wearing big stupid grins.

Next to the photo, in a clean ashtray, is Sammy's wedding ring. I try it on. It's way too big for me. I reach inside my shirt and pull out the string I wear around my neck. On it is the one wedding ring of Chessy's that I didn't pawn. I hold both rings in the palm of my hand. Then I return Sammy's ring and tuck Chessy's back underneath my shirt where it can't be seen.

I start to clean the house. It's the least I can do for Sammy. Besides, the Santa Anas are coming. I find a well-stocked closet full of cleaning supplies and begin with the downstairs, then the main level — the living room, dining room, kitchen, and TV room. Sammy has the same TV as Jake, only bigger. Upstairs, I clean the bathrooms, but leave the office and bedroom alone. I don't want it seem like I was prying.

Has it been four hours since I started? As I'm putting the things away, I hear a key in the door. Maybe Willow is back from her audition. The door opens and a lady in a Metallica sweatshirt and jeans comes in. She looks like the Russian grandmother on the Pizza Palace commercials.

"Oh! Excuse me."

"Excuse me," I echo.

She clearly knows her way around the house.

"I'm Maybe," I tell her.

"Maybe what?"

"Maybe, that's my name."

"Maybe your name's what?"

"Never mind."

"Fine." She heads straight to the kitchen and starts filling up a bucket of water.

"Are you one of the Santa Anas?"

"No, I am Vilma."

"Wilma?"

"Vilma! The housekeeper."

I let this sink in. "I just cleaned the house," I say, gesturing around the room.

Vilma makes clucking noises with her tongue. "Mr. Sammy, he hired you?"

"No, I'm a . . . guest."

"That's fine. But this is my job. I clean. You, go away, shoo! I busy! No time to talk, talk, talk! Scoot!"

I head out. I'm not sure where I am going, but I can't hang around here.

## ★ TWENTY-EIGHT ★

I hike down the winding street. Some houses are all bunched together; others are set apart by empty lots overgrown with weeds. One house is for sale. A plastic tube hangs off the sign. I take out a flyer and choke. The asking price is over three million dollars, and it's a dump. I wonder what Sammy's house is worth.

As I make my way down the hill, the sound of traffic gets louder. There are more fancy cars flying down this narrow stretch of highway than in all of Florida.

I'm hungry. I don't see any restaurants, but I do spot a construction site in the distance. There is a truck parked nearby that says, BENITO'S TACOS #4 on the side in fancy lettering. It looks good to me.

The girl in the taco truck is clearly cleaning up to go. She looks down from the window. "Can I help you?"

"Are you still serving?"

"Well, officially, no. But I can make you something. What would you like?"

"A taco?"

"What kind?"

I look at the menu. It's all in Spanish. *Carne asada? Carnitas? Al pastor?*

"Can I just have a plain taco?"

She laughs, but not in a mean way. "One plain taco coming up."

The girl dumps some meat on the grill. By now I'm starving, and the sizzling sound is more beautiful than any music I have ever heard. In one move, she scoops the meat up and places it on two small tortillas, then sprinkles some green stuff on it and some onions.

"Guacamole?"

"Sure, why not?"

She hands it to me on a paper plate. It looks nothing like what I get at Taco Bell. I pay her and sit on one of the plastic lawn chairs nestled in the dirt. I can see the ocean in the distance. I pick up my taco and take a bite. Instantly, my taste buds go on overload. The meat is tender and juicy and the onions are just right. It's like there's a party in my mouth.

"Thisissogood!"

The girl laughs again. "*Carnitas*," she tells me. "You want another taco?"

"Sure!"

"How about *al pastor* this time?"

"Bring it on!"

Four tacos and a soda later I am ready to burst. "That last one's on the house," the girl tells me. She smiles a lot and has the whitest teeth I have ever seen. "I had fun watching you eat." She climbs down from the truck and sits down next to me. "Do you live around here?" she asks as she sips a green soda from a bottle.

"Temporarily," I tell her. "Do you?"

"No way," she laughs. "I live in East L.A. Not in a million years could we afford this zip code."

She tosses her soda bottle in the trash can and I do the same with mine. Then we both pick up trash around the truck.

"You don't have to do that."

"I don't have anything better to do."

The girl seems to be about my age, maybe a couple years older. She has thick black hair that's pulled back in a ponytail, a deep tan, no makeup, and a beautiful smile. She's way prettier than any of Chessy's Charmers.

"Well, I have to go," she tells me. "I had fun talking to you. Most of my customers are construction guys and when they aren't hitting on me, they're telling each other crude jokes. I hope I see you again."

"Tomorrow," I promise. "By the way, what's your name?"

"I'm Jessica Consuelo Guadalupe Morales Lopez, but you can call me Jess."

I start to laugh but stop when I see a look of embarrassment cross her face. "No, no, it's not you," I insist. "It's just that my name is Maybelline Mary Katherine Mary Ann Chestnut, but you can call me Maybe."

Jess flashes a smile. "*Hasta mañana*, Maybe!"

## ★ TWENTY-NINE ★

**S**ammy comes home happy. As I recall, he was generally in a good mood except when my mother was drinking. Nobody was happy then. We are setting the table when Sammy says, "I made some phone calls today. I got you a job as a nanny!"

"Great!" I try to look enthusiastic.

Sammy looks around. "The house looks nice. Maybe, did you meet Vilma?"

Willow sits down, waiting to be served. It's take-out sushi.

"I started to clean so the house would look nice for the Santa Anas," I tell Sammy, "but then your housekeeper showed up."

Willow begins to snicker.

"The Santa Anas?" Sammy asks.

"Willow said they were coming to visit," I say defensively.

Willow sucks in a deep breath and then howls, "Santa Anas? Santa Anas? The Santa Ana WINDS!"

I feel my face burn red.

"The Santa Anas," Sammy explains, trying to stifle his smile, "are high dry winds that we get in Southern California. When they come, everyone gets a little crazy."

"Are you kidding?" Willow is now choking from laughing so

hard. I hope she dies. "Everyone goes nuts when the Santa Anas come. It's like the whole town goes bonkers!"

"Hey," Sammy says softly. "It was really nice of you to help clean, but you don't need to do that, Maybe. Your babysitting gig will begin next week. Tessa, the mom, wants to meet you before then, okay?"

"Sure. Whatever."

I stare at the sushi as Sammy puts it on plates. Babysitting? Wait until Ted hears about this.

## ★ THIRTY ★

"And this is Tammy and this is Todd and this is Tina; they're triplets."

"And you're Tessa?"

"Right. I'm the mommy."

Right. The triplets are staring at me. They all have curly brown hair like their mother. One is picking her nose. One is tugging on her ear. One is making a funny face.

"I make poop poop," the boy shouts gleefully.

"Good for you, Todd!" Tessa claps and carries him off.

The two girls continue to stare at me as I stand in the entryway. Would it be rude to bolt? Both girls are dressed as ballerinas, only they are carrying small plastic baseball bats. One whacks me in the knee. I am about to turn around and run when I hear Tessa yell, "Maybe, come on in. Be sure to lock the door. The kids think it's funny to wander off. I've got 911 programmed into speed dial. Just press #47."

I wade through a sea of toys. There is a beautiful glass coffee table in the living room with diapers duct-taped to each corner. Tessa returns sipping a juice box. "Drink?" she says, handing me one. Todd runs through the room wearing only a Lakers jersey. "Todd! Where is your diaper?" Tessa cries. "Excuse me."

The girls are staring with their mouths hanging open. One points to my hair. "Fire? Hair fire?"

"No, it's just red."

"Red!" the other one squeals, pointing to her sparkly red shoes.

"Yes, red."

Tessa is smiling when she comes back with Todd in tow. He is fully dressed, although he's only wearing one shoe and it looks like it's on the wrong foot. "I see you're already getting along great with the girls!" Tessa gushes as she adjusts her headband. "I was so thrilled when Sammy called. He's such a nice man. Very patient. Yes, very patient."

We both turn to admire the family portrait hanging above a massive stone fireplace mantel and share a moment of silence. I recognize Sammy's style. Unobtrusive. Everyone is barefoot, wearing jeans and a white T-shirt. Tessa and her husband look serene. The triplets look calm.

"We could use you every day," Tessa says, flipping open a calendar. Only one of her hands has nail polish on it. "But that would probably kill you." She laughs nervously and blinks several times. "How about five days a week? Monday through Friday, and some weekends if Tim and I have a fund-raiser or something. We can pay you eight dollars an hour, how does that sound? Not enough? Nine dollars? Ten dollars, I'll pay you ten dollars an hour."

I do the math in my head. That's a lot of money.

"Okay, eleven dollars an hour." Todd is now hitting one of his sisters with a naked Barbie doll. She is howling. Tessa pretends nothing is wrong and I do the same.

"Sounds good," I tell her. Already I'm thinking of asking for a raise.

"Marvelous!" Tessa walks me to the door. "You can start on Monday, unless you'd like to start right now?"

"No, no, Monday will be fine."

As she shuts the door I hear a loud crash inside the house, followed by, "Who broke Mommy's crystal vase?"

With nothing else to do, I head down the road. I've been eating at the taco truck every day. Jess is taking orders, cooking, and making change all at the same time. Just watching her makes me feel like a slacker.

A construction worker leers at Jess. "Hey, honey, how much for some of your homemade hot sauce?"

She smiles sweetly and says, "Shove it, jackass, or you're not getting fed." This shuts him up. Jess winks at me. I smile back and pick up trash around the truck and wipe down the chairs. I like keeping busy, and it helps Jess out.

After the lunch crowd has disappeared, Jess fires up the grill just for us. Chorizo this time, extra guacamole, and homemade salsa. I close my eyes as I take the first bite of my taco. The first bite is always the best. We both collapse into the plastic chairs. Jess hands me a pineapple Jarritos soda in a glass bottle. It's sweet, but balances the spiciness of the tacos perfectly.

"How long have you been doing this?" I ask, gesturing to the truck.

"Eight years. I started when I was ten. This is my first summer solo."

"Cool!"

"Yeah, usually it's two people to a truck. But we ran out of relatives," Jess jokes. She takes a swig of her mango soda. As she stares at the beach, Jess says, "My school counselor thought I should go to college."

"What do you think?"

"That I should go to college. I made honor roll every year," she says shyly. "At graduation, I was voted Most Likely to Succeed. I've always wanted to be a lawyer."

"So why don't you go?"

"Because of this," Jess says, holding up a taco. "Uncle Benny convinced my mom that college is a waste of time and the family comes first. He says that if I play my cards right, I will be part owner of his taco-truck empire. Like I really want to do this for the rest of my life."

There's an awkward silence.

"Sammy, my sorta stepdad, says I have to start babysitting, starting Monday. He wants me to work this summer. I think he's afraid that if I don't keep busy I'll get into trouble."

Apparently, when Sammy was my age, he borrowed the neighbor's car for a joyride, got caught, and did time in juvie. "I learned my lesson," he told me. That's where Sammy and Chessy differ. She never learns.

I look at the taco truck gleaming in the sunlight. "I won't be able to come by anymore."

"That's a bummer," Jess says. I can tell she means it.

"Yeah, and you should see these three kids. They're triplets and from what I could tell, they are the spawn of the devil. Unfortunately, I have no choice." I take a bite of taco and chew slowly, savoring the delectable taste of the meat and spices. This will probably be my last taco. How am I going to get through summer without Jess's tacos? But what other choice do I have? Sammy doesn't want me just moping around the house. Plus, I'm thinking of hiring a private detective to find my father, so I'm going to need money.

I watch Jess get up and haul the trash bags into the truck. She works so hard. Wait . . . she works so hard.

"Jess," I call out, "can I work for you?"

"For me?"

"You said it's usually two to a taco truck. You're totally overworked. The line is always really long and those construction workers don't like to wait," I say in a rush. "Oh please, please, please, you wouldn't have to pay me much, and I'd work really hard, I swear."

My heart is racing as Jess takes her time thinking this over. Finally she says, "Uncle Benny would never approve. This is a family-only business and he's suspicious of outsiders."

"Uncle Benny never has to know," I beg. "You can pay me in cash, or in tacos, or whatever. Please, Jess, save me from Tammy and Todd and Tina and Tessa, pleeeeeease . . ."

Jess starts to laugh. "Maybe, groveling doesn't become you. Please let go of my arm."

"I'm not letting go until you say I can work for you."

"Okay, okay!" Jess finally says. "Uncle! You can work for me. You've been helping out so much already, I really should pay you."

I leap up and hug her. "You won't be sorry, I promise."

Jess is still laughing. "See you tomorrow, Maybe. Get here by ten o'clock."

"*Hasta mañana*, Jess!"

## ★ THIRTY-ONE ★

Ted drops by Sammy's house unannounced. "Hollywood was right behind me in the Green Hornet," he says. "It seems like I'm always losing that boy."

A moment later, the doorbell rings. "I'll get it!" Ted yells. "Hey, Hollywood, fancy meeting you here."

Hollywood steps inside and lets out an appreciative whistle as he turns on his camera.

"Hey, Sam," Ted says, slapping Sammy on the back. "This is our good friend Hollywood —"

"Daniel. My name's Daniel."

"Okay, fine. Rewind. Hey, Sam, this is our good friend Daniel," Ted continues. "Be nice to him; he's going to be a famous director someday." Hollywood waves as he pans the room.

If Sammy thinks my friends are strange, he doesn't let on. "Well, we're just on our way out, but you kids have fun. Willow and I are catching a movie."

Ted stares at her. She is wearing super high heels, a short black dress, and a snotty attitude. "You look pretty tonight," he says. "Are you famous?"

"Not yet," she tells him. "But I will be."

"Me too!"

Before Sammy and Willow pull out of the driveway, Hollywood and Ted are already raiding the refrigerator. "Maah says that they're having a special on pistachios at Costco," Ted announces as he munches on mint Oreos. "But Paww says that too many nuts aren't healthy."

"I'm entering my documentary in the First Take student film fest," Hollywood informs us. "I showed one of my professors the rough cut of my film and he suggested it. The finalists get a special screening, and if you win it's a really big deal."

"Well, I have some news too," I say. "I got a job working on a taco truck."

Ted makes a sour face. "A taco truck?"

"We all can't work for once-famous reclusive movie stars, live in mansions, and drive Rolls-Royces."

"True," he muses. "That takes special skills. Miss de la Tour says that I am her most trusted employee, even more than Cook, who's been with her for twenty-five years." Ted dips his cookie in milk. "Have you told Sammy?"

I nod. "He's not too happy, nor is Tessa, the lady with the triplets. But I promised her I'd babysit now and then, and that got her to stop crying for a little while."

Hollywood's channel surfing on Sammy's big TV. He's the only person I know who likes to watch commercials to study the camera angles. "Uh, Maybe, you might be seeing less of me for a while. On top of everything else, I've got to work on my documentary and . . ."

"Just say it, Hollywood. You're sick of me."

"No, no, I never said that. I would never say that! — Honest. In fact, I really ought to be working on my film right now."

"Then go home, Hollywood." I take the remote from his hands. "Finish your documentary. Make us proud."

Hollywood gets misty-eyed. "I do want to make you proud, Maybe."

"Good-bye, Hollywood!" Ted and I both yell.

The door shuts and Ted asks, "What do you think of him?"

"What do you mean, what do I think of him? He's Hollywood."

"I know." Ted takes over the couch. "But do you like him?"

"Ted, he's Hollywood. He's just Hollywood. It's not like he's Nelson B. Nelson or anyone."

"True," Ted muses. "He's nothing like Nelson B. Nelson, who by the way is way too peppy, don't you think?"

I swat Ted with a pillow. "Don't you go talking about my Nelson like that!"

"You can have him!" Ted cries. "He's not my type. By the way, look what I got us . . ."

I can't help but laugh. "Okay, I'll make the popcorn. You put *The Best of Nelson's Neighborhood* into the DVD player."

## ★ THIRTY-TWO ★

I get to the taco truck location early. Jess hasn't arrived yet. I shade my eyes and look out over the ocean. It's beautiful. I can see why people would pay millions of dollars to live here. If I had millions, this is where I'd want to live.

When Benito's Tacos #4 finally pulls up, I run to the truck as Jess jumps out and lifts the side to create an awning. I haul out the trash can and plastic chairs. We have to rush. The construction workers have seen the truck and are making their way toward us. It's only ten A.M., but they start working at six A.M. or sometimes earlier, so they're ready for lunch whenever Jess shows up.

I step inside and am instantly dumbstruck. The truck is a lot bigger than I would have expected. Shiny stainless steel covers the entire interior. There's a large grill, and a stove with four burners, and a double sink. Not an inch of space is wasted. There are compartments everywhere, above and below, and each is full. Rock is on the radio.

"Don't just stand there, Maybe." Jess hands me a T-shirt. "Quick, put this on."

"Why?" I stammer. It looks ten sizes too small.

"Maybe," she says sternly, "if you work at Benito's you have to wear a Benito's shirt."

Reluctantly, I turn my back and take off my Beefy Hanes XL. I don't like the way the new shirt hugs my body. Before I can protest, Jess is tossing tortilla packages to me. "Start opening these and stacking them over there. When you're done with that, take out the meat from the fridge." She turns the heat up on the grill and stirs the onions on the back burner, and we're in business.

The rest of the day goes past in a blur. Jess does all the cooking and order taking. I make change and generally do whatever she tells me. This includes stocking the sodas, topping the tacos with onions and cilantro, and wrapping up the to-go food. We are constantly bumping into each other. I had no idea it was such hard work.

I am too busy to be bothered by the sexist remarks from a couple of the guys, which include jokes about fish tacos, two girls in a truck, and wanting to know if my hair is bright red everywhere. Most of the guys are nice, though, and find the food much more interesting than either Jess or me.

By the end of the day I am exhausted. I smell like tacos and am all sweaty. My feet hurt. I have burns on my arms from grease splatters, and stains all over my shirt.

I love my job.

Jess and I plop down in plastic chairs. She hands me a plate with different meats on it.

"You ready for school?"

"School?"

"Jessica's Taco Cuisine 101! This," she says, pointing, "is *carnitas*." I take a bite and smile. I know carnitas. The marinated roast pork is my favorite. "Tell me, what's this?" she asks, pointing.

"Chicken?"

"We call it *pollo*."

"And this?"

"*Carne asada*, beef."

"And this?"

I take a bite. It's a little chewy, but tasty. "*Al pastor*?"

"*Tripas*. Tripe."

"What's tripe?" I ask, helping myself to more. It sort of reminds me of clams.

"Beef intestines."

"Beef what?"

"Intestines. Beef intestines."

I put that taco down. Jess laughs and hands me a big plastic bag. It's heavy. "Here's today's pay, hope you don't mind cash. Uncle Benny doesn't know I've hired you, nor does the IRS."

I rise and start stacking the chairs.

"Go home, Maybe," Jess orders. "Relax and get ready for tomorrow. I'll clean up."

I'm too tired to protest. As I walk away Jess calls out, "Hey, Maybelline Mary Katherine Mary Ann Chestnut!" I turn around. "You did great!"

I return her grin.

As I trudge up the hill to Sammy's house, the bag gets heavier and heavier. I stop on the side of the road and open it. Thank God, Jess included a Jarritos lime soda. The glass bottle has beads of sweat on it. I twist off the cap and drink greedily. Refreshed, I take out two Benito's shirts and unwrap something in tinfoil.

At first I think it might be tortillas, but it's not. It's forty-two dollars in cash. Jess also packed enough food to last a week.

To my disappointment, Twig is home. (That's my nickname for Willow.) She is either arranging lettuce on a plate or making a meal. I watch with morbid curiosity as she lifts a plastic bottle and sprays her salad.

"Are you trying to kill the bugs?"

"No," she sniffs. "It's salad dressing. This way I don't get too much on it." She looks me up and down. "You're not fat," she says, surprised.

"Who said I was?"

"Well, you're always wearing those hideously large T-shirts, so I just assumed you were hiding your fat."

The baggy clothes were my mother's doing. I was in the seventh grade and we were at the Fashion Square Mall in Orlando. "For heaven's sake, Maybelline, come out of the dressing room," Chessy ordered.

"No way!" I shouted back.

"Don't be silly, come on! I'm not going to quit yelling until you do."

Slowly I stepped out. Chessy took one look at me in a bathing suit and shrieked, "Maybelline Mary Katherine Mary Ann Chestnut, you have boobies! Maybelline, LOOK! You have boobies! Have you been hiding those darlings from me?"

As I recoiled in horror, I could hear her telling strangers. "Oh, I could just cry. My Maybelline has boobies. She's always been so flat, but she has boobies now! I'm so happy I think I'll treat Maybelline and her boobies to Dairy Queen!"

That's the day I started wearing baggy T-shirts.

"Your makeup is runny," Chessy is saying. No wait, it's Twig. "And you look scary."

When I go to the bathroom I am horrified by what I see. My eyes looked smudged, like a raccoon.

It feels good to take a shower. I slip into fresh clothes, then head back upstairs. Twig's eyes widen as I take out my haul. The delicious smell of tacos fills the room. I eat slowly to torture Twig as she pokes at her salad.

"There's plenty here," I say as I chew slowly. "Would you like some?"

"No, thank you. I'm fine."

Sammy has a big *People* magazine shoot in San Francisco. He's gone for five days, leaving me and Twig alone together. We hardly talk. Instead, she slouches around the house and I try to fade into the background. It's weird. She's closer to my age than Sammy's. I don't like looking at her because she reminds me of my mother, only without the big hair and big personality. In fact, she seems devoid of personality. I don't know what Sammy sees in her. Well, except for Chessy.

We're pretty good at avoiding each other. Still, sometimes accidents happen.

"You're just living off of him," Twig is saying as she spears her lettuce.

"You're the freeloader," I shoot back.

Twig opens her mouth then shuts it, like a ventriloquist's dummy. Finally, she answers, "I am not freeloading. I plan to help with the mortgage once I get some acting gigs. Besides, Sammy's my boyfriend and he likes that I'm living here. He doesn't like to be alone."

That's true. When he was my stepdad, he always wanted company. Even if he was just watching television, he'd always say, "Maybe, come join me." And I would, because I liked that he asked, and I wanted to spend time with him and pretend he was my real dad.

Toward the end of Chessy and Sammy's marriage, the second one, it seemed like Sammy and I were spending more time with each other than with my mother. Chessy was too busy with her pageants and charm school and booze to hang around with us.

". . . I have an audition for a baked beans commercial." Has Twig been talking all this time? "My agent says I am perfect for the part."

"Goodie," I say.

As Twig attacks her lettuce, I wonder how long Chessy's been on a diet. The only time she's ever off it is on her wedding days when she has a slice of wedding cake. I guess she'll be able to go off her diet in a month or so when she marries Jake. I can't believe she's going through with it.

Suddenly I'm not hungry anymore.

# ★ THIRTY-THREE ★

**H**ollywood's slaving over his documentary. This film competition is a big deal to him. Still, he calls me every night when he takes a break. From what I can tell, film students are like doctors. They work around the clock without sleep. Hollywood will babble on and on about nothing, but when I ask him about his film he clams up. He's superstitious. Like when his mom had her second cancer operation, he didn't want to discuss it. Instead, I sat with him for hours while we listened to Ted spout off about whatever popped into his head.

So, Hollywood's working. Sammy's in San Francisco. And Ted's in Las Vegas with Miss de la Tour — apparently she's some sort of high roller when it comes to the craps table. But that's okay. I have Benito's Taco Truck #4 and Jess.

The first hundred dollars went to pay Parker back. "Be sure to give this to him," I instructed Hollywood. "And tell him that the extra twenty dollars is for him to buy something for his daughter." I also owe Ted and Hollywood a ton of money, plus I want to return the money I took from Ian. And I want to get something nice for Sammy since he refuses to take anything for rent or food. I'm saving the rest for a private detective.

Though it's only been a few days, Jess and I have a routine worked out. She takes the orders, I prep the food, she cooks. I take the money, she serves. We both clean up. We do this a hundred times a day. At least that's what it feels like. I'm starting to recognize the guys. There's Toby, who always orders carne asada tacos, no onions. Caesar, who likes his with pollo and extra sour cream. Eric likes his five carnitas tacos without cilantro. Everyone drinks Jarritos.

A couple of cops have lunch at the truck every day too. We never charge them.

"There are lots of laws about taco trucks, but if the police like you, they don't mind looking the other way," Jess informs me as she bags their tacos and slips in extra salsa and guacamole.

"Like what kind of laws?"

"Like you can't be at one spot for too long."

"That's stupid."

"That's the law."

"Who'd make a law like that?"

"The restaurant owners," Jess says as she slices limes. She's so fast she could be on one of those Ginsu knife commercials. "We're competition, so it pays to feed the cops and get to know them. My mom's terrified I'm going to get arrested some day, and they'll take me away from her."

I laugh. "That's my mother's dream come true."

The onions I'm chopping are making me start to tear up.

"When was the last time you and your mom got along?" Jess asks.

I stop to think. "Well, one Christmas we stayed up late and decorated the tree with chains we made out of construction paper. And we ate gingerbread cookies made by the mom of one of her beauty pageant contestants, and we both fell asleep on the couch. In the morning, there were presents under the tree and Chessy cooked pancakes for breakfast."

"When was that?"

"I don't know. When I was really little."

"What about your dad?"

"Which one? I've had several. Actually, I came to Los Angeles to find my biological father. He doesn't even know I'm alive."

Jess mops her forehead with a paper towel. "I can't believe you came all this way to look for him. I've never been out of Southern California. You're really brave, Maybe."

Me, brave? I thought I was a coward to run away.

"Why would anyone want to leave here?" I say, motioning to the beach.

"To know," she says wistfully. "Just to see. I always thought it would be cool to go to college back East. But we can't afford it, plus I don't want to leave my mom. My mother left Mexico when she was a teenager. We're trying to get my grandmother to move here, but she doesn't want to. My mom cries for her all the time and says a prayer for her every day. She sees her once a year when she goes home."

When I get back to Sammy's I sit on my bed and look around the room. Sammy's said that I can redecorate if I want to, but so far nothing's changed. I wonder what my biological father's house looks like. I've kept looking for him on Sammy's computer, but I don't have any more leads today than I had yesterday.

I stare at the photo of my mom and me and Sammy. We all look so happy. What went wrong?

I wonder what my mother is doing right now. Is she thinking about me?

I pick up the phone and take a deep breath before dialing. A familiar voice picks up.

"Hello? Hello?"

"Hi, it's me, Maybe."

"Maybe? Where are you, hon?"

In a rush I tell Ridgeway about running away, and living in the dorms, and meeting up with Sammy, and working on the taco truck.

"Whoa, whoa, slow down, girl, or you'll get me dizzy," he says, chuckling.

I realize I have been talking about myself nonstop for ten minutes, when the real reason I called was to ask questions.

"Ridgeway . . . ?"

"Yes, darling."

"How is she? Does she even care that I'm gone?"

Ridgeway is silent for a moment, but it feels like an eternity. I brace myself.

"She's a basket case, Maybe. With you leaving and her pageant princesses bailing on her, she's hitting the bottle quite hard."

"And Jake?"

"Yeah, he's still around, but they fight all the time."

Now it's my turn to be silent.

"Maybe? Are you still there?"

"I'm still here," I finally say. "Ridgeway, Jake tried to rape me. Chessy doesn't believe me. That's why I left."

"Oh, Maybelline, I am so sorry," Ridgeway says softly. "I believe you."

"Do you think she misses me at all?"

"I do, in her own way. But she's mastered that jaw-locking beauty pageant smile that can cover up anything. Your momma was always very good at that. You want me to tell her you called?"

"No, please don't do that." I hesitate, then ask, "Do you remember anything about my biological father? His name? Anything?"

"Sorry, Maybe. I met your mother just after he left her. She's never mentioned anything about him. I think she's ashamed." I feel my face flush. "Oh, darling," he's quick to add, "not of you, of him leaving her."

"Look after Chessy, will you?" I tell him. "I know what it's like when she drinks."

"I'm no substitute for you, but I'll do my best."

"Thanks, Ridgeway."

I hang up and stare out the window. My mother drinks to forget. The minute Sammy left for California, Chessy started drinking hard. She never did intend for us to join him.

Is it me she's trying to forget now?

## ★ THIRTY-FOUR ★

It's Sunday. I have the day off since Jess and I don't work weekends. Sammy's San Francisco gig went well. He just wanted to chill, but Twig talked him into taking her to Catalina Island for a couple days. Sammy invited me, but I told him I had to work tomorrow. Twig beamed when she heard this.

Ted's back from Las Vegas and we're going out to lunch. He's even talked Hollywood into taking some time off to come with us.

"Mademoiselle . . ." Hollywood bows as he opens the back door of the Rolls. He's such a nerd. On the seat is a Viva Las Vegas snow globe that's as big as a cantaloupe.

"That's yours!" Ted looks pleased with himself. "I was going to get you jewelry, but this seemed more you."

"You look different." Hollywood reaches for his Super 8. "What did you do?"

"*Beeeep!*" Ted shouts. "What is no makeup and no baggy clothes?" He's always wanted to go on *Jeopardy!*

"Why the makeover?" Hollywood asks from behind the camera. "Not that it isn't an improvement."

Ted turns around to check me out. "She looks a thousand

times better! Now if only we could do something about the hair."

"I've always liked the hair," Hollywood says. "It's spunky. Very *Sid and Nancy*. Not many people could carry that off. You have to have a certain *joie de vivre*."

"What's *joie de vivre*?" I ask.

"It's French for *love of life*," Hollywood explains as Ted maneuvers down the street.

"Ah, *français*," Ted says with a contented sigh. "I've always felt a kinship toward the French. They have excellent pastries. Speaking of tarts, don't you think Maybe's hair color is over the top?"

"Anything's better than my hair," Hollywood says glumly. "One time I went to one of those barber colleges where they'll cut your hair for free just for the chance to practice on a real person. Only everyone refused to work on me. Maybe's hair is a product of her own creativity, even if it does look weird."

"STOP! Do you idiots realize that I can hear you?" I shout.

As Hollywood and Ted continue critiquing my appearance, I look out the window and watch the coast whiz past. It's like an endless postcard. Hills and tall palm trees on one side, beaches swarming with bronzed sunbathers and surfers on the other.

Since I started working on the taco truck, I've stopped wearing makeup. It just melts off anyway. Out of habit I put on a Benito's shirt every morning. Jess also lent me some shorts, which I have to admit are more comfortable than jeans when you're working in what's essentially a metal box on wheels. The small portable fan does little to cool us off. When customers aren't looking, Jess and I stick our hands into cups of crushed ice.

By the time we get to Santa Monica, Hollywood's talking about his student film competition again. "It's a big deal." He pauses and then says, "A REALLY big deal." He raises his eyebrows for emphasis.

"Miss de la Tour won big in Vegas," Ted informs us. "She always wins."

"To even be a finalist looks great on your resume," Hollywood muses.

"You should have seen the buffets — they go on for miles."

"A USC student has won the last five years in a row."

"Ever wonder why they call them crap tables?"

At least they aren't the kind of guys who talk sports all the time, like some of Chessy's exes. Sammy's not big into sports, though he likes to play tennis. Carlos was a jock. His sport was baseball and he played in a league. Jake's sport is, of course, bowling. That and lying.

Ted pulls up to some run-down restaurant called The Seaside Shack. I am surprised when a valet appears out of nowhere to park the Rolls. The hostess seats us on the patio. We're practically on the beach. Her eyes move down to Ted's shoes. She smirks, then asks, "Would you like a children's menu?"

He offers her a sweet smile and replies, "Would you like brain augmentation?"

"My treat," I announce as I pick up the menu. My jaw drops. For the price of an entree you could get twelve tacos, a large side of guacamole, and three Jarritos. Ted is more interested in food than economics. I've noticed that ever since he started hanging out with Gloria de la Tour, his tastes have gotten expensive. He orders the soft-shell crabs, calamari salad, and a side of garlic fries. Hollywood gets a cheeseburger and so do I. We split an order of fries and when asked what we'd like to drink, we both insist, "Water's fine."

"Thanks," I mouth to Hollywood.

"You're welcome," he mouths back.

After lunch we walk to the beach. It's the first time I have ever stepped foot on the sand. It's burning hot, so I run to the water and let it wash over my toes. It feels wonderful. Ted refuses to take off his platform shoes and promptly falls in a hole.

"Help! Quicksand!"

"Oh my God," Hollywood shouts. "Look at that!" He rushes toward Ted and starts filming. Finally, when Ted throws sand at him, he stops and pulls him out as I stand on the sidelines laughing.

"Hey, I have a brilliant idea," Ted says as he sits on the curb pouring the sand out of his shoes. "Let's take Maybe shopping. I'm getting tired of having to look at her in the same old clothes all the time."

"I'm in," Hollywood says. Apparently he hasn't noticed that he's fashion-challenged.

"Isn't anyone going to ask me how I feel about this?"

"NO!" they yell at the same time.

We head to the Third Street Promenade with its street performers and boutiques and restaurants. The first store we go into has taken mood lighting too seriously. It is so dark I can barely see the clothes. The salesgirls don't even acknowledge us, preferring to gossip about some celebrity whose liposuction destroyed her thighs and her career.

Near the register, Hollywood is fascinated by a basket filled with small slips of colorful material. "Are these hospital masks?" he asks as he rifles through them.

One of the girls smirks. "They're women's thongs. I don't think we have them in your size."

I don't have to look at Hollywood to know that he's turning red.

"Let's get out of here," Ted says loudly. "We'll spend our family fortunes elsewhere."

As we exit, the sun blinds us all. I squint to make out the building in front of us. "There," I say, marching toward it. "That's where we need to be."

Once inside the mall I spot a Shah's department store. I herd the guys toward it. Ted's hyper like a baby goat and Hollywood's acting like an ancient giraffe, so it takes a while. Out of habit, I head to the men's department until Ted booms, "Halt! Back up. It's Teen Scene for you, missy!"

I half seriously/half jokingly fight Hollywood and Ted as they drag me toward the brightly colored dresses and flowered tops in the junior girls' department. "Sit here," Ted orders, pushing me into a chair near the dressing room. He turns to Hollywood. "Let's fan out, gather some clothes, and meet back here in fifteen minutes."

They coordinate watches. A middle-aged man with a so-so toupee is slouched in the chair across from me. Resting on his lap is a woman's brown leather handbag. His eyelids keep slowly opening and closing, like he's trying to stay awake. I smile at him. He smiles back, then gives up and nods off, snoring lightly.

Hollywood is the first to return from his mission. He is carrying several pairs of shorts that look like khaki versions of the denim ones Jess has been lending me. "I didn't know your size," he says apologetically. He also hands me some T-shirts emblazoned with photos of retro bands, and a flimsy yellow sundress that I know I won't be wearing.

Ted bounds toward us with a white bathing suit and some jeans. He hands me a pink bathrobe. "Look," he says proudly. "It's festooned with bunnies! Festooned!"

I slip on a pair of shorts first. They are nice, but too big. The third pair fits, and so do all the T-shirts. They're snug, like my Benito's ones, but I sort of like the way they look on me. Since I've been working on the taco truck, my body is toned for the first time in my life. I'm even tanned. I note that I will need a new bra, and some new panties wouldn't hurt. Vilma left a note on mine after she washed them: *Keep, toss, or burn?*

I ignore the sundress and move on to the jeans. They fit perfectly, but are expensive. I walk out to show the guys.

The man with the purse is awake and Ted is explaining, "She's been dressing like a boy for so long, we thought we'd do a kind of makeover on her."

"Oh, like on that show *Queer Guys for the Straight Gal?*"

"What are you trying to say?" Ted asks.

Hollywood's camera is rolling. "How do you feel wearing clothes that actually fit?" he asks me.

"Am I going to be on television?" The man adjusts his hair and tucks the purse under the chair.

"Maybe, you have a butt!" Ted exclaims.

I try to look angry, but can't help myself and smile. "I'm taking these," I say, pointing to the jeans and T-shirt. "But I still need shorts."

"What's wrong with the ones I gave you?" Hollywood looks hurt.

"Khaki?"

"Yawn. This is boring," Ted declares. "Let's go clothes shopping for someone more interesting, like me. Come on, Hollywood."

As Ted and Hollywood head toward the children's department, I am left alone with the man holding the purse. He shuts his eyes and goes back to sleep. A salesgirl comes over. She's wearing trendy librarian glasses and a cool top that looks all distressed.

"Your dad looks bored."

"He's not my dad."

She laughs. "Well, someone's dad looks bored. I love your hair. Jamaica Kool-Aid?"

I nod.

"Can I help you find anything?"

"I'd like a new look," I confess. "But nothing too girly or frou-frou. And I don't like clothes that are too tight or revealing. And I don't like bright colors or things with patterns. And I don't like glittery clothes, or clothes that are complicated, and I hate —" I cover my mouth when I realize that I have been babbling.

"I think we have the same taste," the salesgirl tells me. "Here's a tip. Go to Aaardvark's on Melrose in Hollywood. You'll find what you're looking for there. It's all vintage, plus a lot cheaper than here. But you should get those jeans — they look great on you. They show off your figure."

I pay and head back outside with my bags. Ted and Hollywood are on the Promenade listening to some street musicians playing upturned garbage cans. Ted looks like he's had a bad reaction to lunch, but that's just the way he dances. Hollywood is filming.

A little ways down, a slight gray-haired woman sits at a card table. She's wearing a heavy red velvet robe, even though it must be ninety degrees, and has rings on every finger. Her hand-lettered sign reads, MADAME G. POUPON, FORTUNE TELLER. When she sees me staring, she puts down her Starbucks. "Twenty dollars," she says in a gravelly voice.

I turn to walk away.

"Fifteen dollars," she calls after me. When I keep walking, she yells, "Ten dollars and no less. You're cheating me!"

I sit on the metal folding chair. It's burning hot, but I try to ignore it. Madame Poupon pushes some cards around on the table, which is covered with red velvet. I'll bet she got a good deal on the material. She shuts her eyes and hums, slowly rocking back and forth. I wonder if she remembers I am here. Finally she blinks and stares at me. I shift in my seat.

"You have been on a journey?" I nod. "But you still have far to go. You have a lot of stress on your shoulders. Life is giving you pressure. You are confused."

Madame Poupon could be saying this stuff about anyone. I have just wasted ten dollars. As I get up to leave, she grabs my wrist. "WAIT!" She closes her eyes and begins humming again. "You think that if you find your father, your problems will be solved. But that's not the answer. The answer is . . . the answer is . . ."

"What's the answer? What is it?"

She smiles as her eyes flutter open. "Your time is up. For fifty dollars, I will give you the answer."

"Forget it," I say, shaking my head. "I don't want to know."

## THIRTY-FIVE

It's been days since I've seen Madame Poupon, but I can't stop thinking about what she said. Should I have paid the fifty dollars? Was she telling me not to look for my father? I take out my father file and stare at the photo. How many Gunnars could there be in this town? My internet searches take me nowhere. I've found several shows and movies that were filmed in Florida about the time my father was there, but Gunnar's name never shows up. It's like he never existed.

I finally called a private detective who specializes in finding missing persons.

"What's his full name?" she asked.

"His last known address?"

"Driver's license number?"

"Place of employment?"

"Date of birth?"

"Friends' names?"

"I don't suppose you have his social security number?"

There isn't much I could tell her. "What do you charge?" I asked.

"Honey, let me give you some advice for free." I pressed the phone closer to my ear. "Just ask your mother who he is. If she still won't tell you, my rate is one hundred and fifty dollars an hour with an eight-hour minimum."

The lunch crowd has cleared and Jess and I are taking a breather. "Who are they?" Jess asks, looking over my shoulder.

"My parents."

She takes the photo from my hand. "Your mom's pretty. Is that one of your stepdads?"

"That's my biological father, the one I'm looking for."

Jess stares at the photo for a long time before handing it back to me. "I hope you find him, Maybe. I never knew my dad either."

"What happened to him?"

"He died when I was little."

I turn to ask her about it, but she's already picking up trash outside of the truck.

When I get home, I tuck the photo back into my father file.

Tonight Sammy is taking me out to dinner. Just me. No Twig. "Wear something nice," he says cheerfully as I head downstairs.

Hollywood, Ted, and I really cleaned up at Aaardvark's. Ted found two more pairs of platform shoes, a boy's size XL green corduroy suit, and a fedora. The shoes are women's sizes so they fit him perfectly and he doesn't have to wear three pairs of gym socks. Hollywood scored big-time with a vintage Bruce Lee T-shirt, a 20th Century Fox baseball cap that looks like it's been chewed by a dog, and a red Windbreaker like the one James Dean wore in *Rebel Without a Cause* (only it's all faded and looks more pink than red).

I found two pairs of cutoffs, some ripped jeans, a Boy Scout shirt, and a Hostess Twinkie deliveryman jacket. Ted and I spotted an Andy Warhol scarf at the same time and arm-wrestled for it. Usually he wins, but I really wanted the scarf, so I had Hollywood tickle him. I thought this would make Ted angry, but he didn't seem to mind (although later he claimed I cheated).

I am looking at my clothes spread out on my bed. I only wear my Hanes XL T-shirts to sleep in. I can't believe I used to wear those things in public. There really isn't anything nice enough for me to wear to dinner. I sigh. I know what I have to do, and the thought of it repulses me. But anything for Sammy.

Twig is sitting cross-legged on the couch staring at a fashion magazine. She licks her finger every time she turns the page. I hope she gets a paper cut.

"Hey Willow."

"What?" she says, not bothering to look up.

"Can I borrow some of your clothes?"

That got her attention. She stares at me as if I asked for one of her kidneys.

"No."

"Why not?"

"Yes, why not?" Sammy asks as he walks through the room carrying a camera case. His hair is in a ponytail. He'd look good with an earring.

"Well, er . . . I suppose, if Maybe, well, I guess I can try to find something in her size . . ."

I've been in Willow's closet before. Sometimes when she's not home, Ted and I try on her clothes. Ted's particularly fond of her faux fur. He always growls and pretends to be a bear when he wears it.

As Twig goes through her things, we both already know that

most of them won't fit me. "Well," she finally says as she moves an orange blouse to the fall section of her closet, "you have those new jeans." I am impressed that she knew about them. "Let's pair them with nice shoes and a top, and a great jacket — although, it would be best for you to stay away from patterns or colors that clash with your hair." My hair is blue today.

I look down at my sneakers. They are beyond shredded. Chessy always hated these shoes, which is why I wore them. "Maybelline, something with a defined heel won't kill you," she'd say. "Look what it did for Cinderella."

Twig pulls out a couple of pairs of shoes, including black pointy-toed boots, and several tops. She holds them up in front of my face. "Try these on," she orders. "Put on your good jeans too, so we can see how the ensemble looks."

*The ensemble?* I had no idea she could use three-syllable words.

I have to wriggle to get into my pants. They shrunk the first time I washed them. I try on the black tank top and attempt to slip a fitted jacket over it, but my arm gets stuck so I give up. I wonder if my Hostess Twinkie jacket would qualify as fancy? It's a bit of a struggle, but I get the boots on. At least those fit, although they make me wobbly, like Ted the first time he tried on platform shoes.

Twig is sitting on the bed smoking a cigarette. "The jacket was too small," I tell her, lifting up an arm as proof.

"I'm not surprised."

I am about to insult her skinny skankiness but remember she's doing me a favor. She is now digging through drawers. Finally Twig cries, "Here it is!" and pulls out a sweater.

"It's see-through! I can't wear that!"

"It's the style. Besides, dummy, you wear it over the tank top."

I slip it on. It's nice and roomy, and I actually like the gray color. Twig nods and murmurs, "Not bad, but it needs something."

As she digs through her jewelry box I rush out of the room. "How about this?" I say when I return. I hold up the Andy Warhol scarf.

"Hey, that'll work great."

I begin to tie it around my neck, but Willow starts screaming like she's been shot. "No! No! No! No!" She grabs the scarf from me. "Not there, here!" Willow threads the Warhol through my belt loops. "Like this. There, now you look decent."

I turn to look at myself in the mirror. Twig is right. I do look decent.

"Thank you, Willow."

"Yada, yada, whatever," she answers.

Sammy and I are silent as we ride down the coast in his silver BMW. The top is down and the engine purrs. He always did like nice cars.

We don't do a lot of talking; we never did. But it's not at all uncomfortable. When he was married to Chessy, she talked enough for all of us. We'd both sit in the apartment and listen to her chatter nonstop, then Sammy would take me out for ice cream and we'd sit there contented, savoring our sundaes and the silence.

The restaurant hostess greets Sammy by name and seats us immediately even though there are lots of people ahead of us. "I did her head shots," Sammy whispers. "She's a model."

I'm not surprised. Southern California is the land of the lovely people. All of a sudden I no longer feel like I look decent. I feel lumpy and ugly, like I used to around Chessy's Charmers. I wonder what my mother would think about my looks now.

As if he's reading my mind, Sammy speaks up. "You look wonderful, Maybe. But then, you always did. You got good genes from your mom."

I know he's just being nice.

"So tell me," he continues, "why exactly are you here? What haven't you told me, Maybe?"

I marvel that he waited this long to ask. But then, Sammy has always been very patient. I can't tell him that I'm looking for my biological father. It might hurt his feelings. He's the closest thing to a real father that I've ever had. So instead I quip, "Just wanting to see what the rest of the world is like." The waiter refills my water glass. Sammy doesn't say anything. "I needed to get away," I confess. "It was suffocating in Kissimmee. You used to live there, you know what it's like."

"Why don't you tell me?"

Before I can stop myself I am crying into my artichoke dip. "Jake . . . he tried to . . ."

I stop.

"He tried to what?" I can't stand the way he's looking at me. "What, Maybe?" Sammy says. "Did he do something to you?"

"No. Sort of. Not really." I take a sip of water. It feels cold going down my throat. "Forget it."

Sammy composes himself and tries another tactic. "You can tell me, Maybe. You know that I have always been on your side."

I do know that. We've been hurt by the same person.

"Nothing bad happened," I tell him. "I mean, nothing serious.

Not that he didn't try." I pause. "Well, one really bad thing happened."

Sammy gets all worry-faced again. "What?"

The waiter appears. "Steak, medium rare for you, sir! And roasted chicken for the young lady!"

Sammy and I are frozen until the he leaves.

"She didn't believe me," I whisper. "She chose him instead of me."

Sammy winces.

"I'm so sorry, Maybe." He knows what it's like to be dismissed by Chessy.

We stumble through small talk when really it feels like Chessy is dominating the conversation. Finally I ask, "Sammy, why did you and my mom divorce?"

"The first time or the second time?"

"Both."

He signals the waiter and orders a glass of wine. I've never seen him drink before. When it arrives, he swirls it around and stares at it, like Madame Poupon with her tarot cards.

"The first time, I left her because she refused to stop drinking," he says slowly. "I thought that the threat of me leaving would be enough, but it wasn't. I didn't like what it was doing to her, to me, to you. She'd black out. Do you remember?"

I nod. How could I forget?

"Still, I'd check on you all the time. Then one day I was surprised when Chessy's new husband answered the door. I kept my distance after that. It was too hard on all of us when I showed up."

"What about the second time? How did you two get together again after that?"

"You don't remember?"

I shake my head.

"After Chessy left Jim Marshall, you called me. You were only six or seven years old, but you called and asked me to marry your mother again."

I don't remember.

"So I came back and worked really hard at getting Chessy sober, and we remarried. Shortly afterward I started getting more and more photography jobs and my career kept taking me to California. I should have been around more, but I wasn't.

"Still, Chessy was thrilled for me, for all of us, when we decided to move to Los Angeles. She claimed that she always wanted to live here. However, right before I left, your mom picked a huge fight. She accused me of wanting to leave her, which we both knew was ridiculous." Sammy pauses and shakes his head. "I hoped that it was just the alcohol talking and that once her head cleared everything would be all right. Maybe, your mother's really strong. But sometimes even strong people need help. I thought I could be the one to help her.

"So I came out, scouted good school districts, bought this house, and set up my business. Then one day the doorbell rang. But instead of you and your mother showing up on my doorstep, I was served divorce papers."

Sammy looks pained and I'm sorry for making him relive this, but I need to know. He's not the only one who was hurt. "What was her excuse for not coming?"

"She said she met someone else." Sammy takes a long sip of wine. "Did she?"

"Not right away."

There is a sad silence between us. Finally I ask, "What is it about her? I mean, for you to marry her twice? For all those other men to fall in love with her, when she treats everyone so badly?"

Sammy looks surprised that his wine glass is empty. The waiter materializes and offers him a second glass. Sammy waves him away. "Your mother," he says, carefully selecting his words, "can be intoxicating. When she pays attention to you, you feel like the most important person in the world."

I know what he means.

"I know she can be frustrating," Sammy continues, "but Chessy can also be kind and loving, if you let her. She's not as tough as she thinks she is." He pauses, then chuckles. "I don't suppose you know of a support group for men who have been tossed aside by Chessamay Chestnut."

That's Sammy for you. He looks devastated, yet he's trying to make me feel better.

"I'm sorry," I tell him. The tears burn as they run down my face.

"Me too," he replies.

★　★　★

It's past midnight and I can't sleep.

When I was little and couldn't sleep, my mother would sit on the edge of the bed and tell me stories about her beauty pageant days. Back then, she used to put me in those Little Miss dresses and, get this — I actually won a couple of beauty pageants.

I remember one time Grandma came down from Gainesville to watch me compete. "You gotta win this one," my mom whispered as she sprayed my hair with Aqua Net. "You just have to."

I came in fifth, despite my mother having an "in" with the head judge. It was probably my lack of talent that sealed it. Statistics have shown that puppet shows rarely do well at beauty pageants. Later I switched to a mime act. What other choice did I have? I couldn't sing. I couldn't dance. I couldn't play a musical instrument. Sadly, as a mime, I couldn't even keep quiet.

"Pity about Maybelline," Grandma said as she reapplied her lipstick. She had treated us to Kountry Buffet for dinner. It was all-you-could-eat and they had chocolate pudding and pies and cakes. Grandma only had fruit cocktail and cottage cheese on her tray. "Chessamay, she's on the pudgy side, like you."

I could see my mother stiffen. "I'm not fat," she said as she put back a slice of pie.

"I know you're not, dear," Grandma said sympathetically. "But you were, and inside your body is still a chubby Chessamay fighting to get out. You look better now, although I liked your hair when it was longer. It'll grow, though, so there's nothing to worry about."

Then Grandma turned to me. "Maybelline, darling, stop shoveling those desserts into your mouth. You don't want to get chubby the way your mommy was, do you?"

I put my spoon down and shook my head.

"Now, I've got some pointers for Maybelline," Grandma said, taking out a list. "Shall we go over them now?"

"Let's not, Mother," Chessy said, pushing the list away.

"But these are helpful."

"No, they're not."

"Well, I never!"

Grandma was always saying, "Well, I never!" When I was little I couldn't figure out what she never did. I couldn't figure out Grandma either. One time I asked my mother, "Grandma doesn't like me, does she?"

I waited for my mother to tell me I was wrong, but instead she said, "Grandma doesn't like surprises." Then she wiped my face with a tissue and said, "But I do!"

I liked it when Grandma visited. Not because I liked Grandma; I didn't. What I liked was that when she was around, my mom and I were on the same side.

The next morning Chessy's photos are gone. The walls are bare. Twig is beaming. "I don't know what you said to him last night, but thank you!"

Even though I hated looking at the photos, it makes me sad not to see them anymore.

## ★ THIRTY-SIX ★

**W**hen the house is empty I use Sammy's computer. His screen saver is a photo of my mother. He must have missed that one when he purged the house of Chessy photos.

My search for my father isn't moving forward, so instead, I go backward. I re-contact all the birth family sites and give them the only new information I have: my e-mail address. Sammy set it up for me. He also taught me how to play games on the computer, and I find myself spending more and more time doing that than searching for my biological father. My favorite game is called Dog Detective. Using the clues provided, you search for lost pets. So far, I've rescued twelve dogs.

Hollywood e-mails me a dozen times a day with updates about his film ("It's going great"), messages from his roommate ("Ian says hi"), and general weirdness ("What's the difference between God and a director? God doesn't think he's a director").

Ted looks over my shoulder and reads the latest e-mail from Hollywood. "He never e-mails me," Ted pouts.

"You don't even have an e-mail address," I remind him.

"I could get one."

Ted's totally consumed with his job. "I'm going to have to stop going to the Brentwood Thai Culture Club meetings," he announces as he points the remote toward the TV and races through the channels. "It's a pity since I've just been elected sergeant at arms."

I stop cracking pistachios. "I didn't even know you were a member of the Thai Culture Club."

"Ah, Miss Maybe, there's so much about me you don't know. I'm a man of mystery and I'm totally in demand. Miss de la Tour depends on me for everything."

Ted holds his arm out under my nose. His Mickey Mouse watch is gone and in its place is an expensive-looking watch that's way too big for him. I pretend not to see it. It would make Ted too happy if I noticed it.

"Recently, I've started sitting in with her agent," he says. "We're negotiating for her to appear in a cameo of a prequel to *The Poseidon Adventure.*"

"You should tell this to Hollywood."

"I did."

Since when did he start telling Hollywood things before me?

Sammy strides through the living room. Twig is slouching behind him. "You kids want to go with us to get something to eat?"

When Twig hears this, she looks alarmed. Ted saunters over and holds his wrist under Sammy's nose.

"Nice watch."

"Oh, you noticed! Miss de la Tour gifted me with it. It's an antique Rolex and it used to belong to one of her husbands. She's been married almost as many times as Maybe's mom. Hey! Where are all the Chessy photos?"

There is an awkward silence as the question hangs in the air. Sammy scoops up his keys from the front-door table. "Well, we're leaving. Guess we'll see you when we get back."

"That was weird," Ted says, still staring at the blank walls.

"You jerk."

"What? What did I do?"

I just shake my head. "Are we going to the movies or what?"

Ted lights up. "I thought we'd go to the Rialto theater and see *Life with Aubrey and Andy*."

"I've never heard of it. Is it new?"

"It's old, and it stars the fabulous Gloria de la Tour. She was nominated for an Oscar for that one, but Audrey Hepburn won." I start to tell Ted that I once shared a sandwich with a different Audrey Hepburn, but he keeps going. "I told Miss de la Tour I'd check it out, see how many people are there. You know, give her a full report."

I grab my Hostess Twinkies jacket and we're on our way. When Ted turns on the engine, a familiar voice says, *"Voilà la porte!"* Startled, I look around.

"Miss de la Tour plans to go to Paris for the fall," Ted explains as he turns down the volume on the CD player. "I figured she'll probably want me to go too, so I should learn to speak the language. *Comprenez-vous?* These are those CDs they're always advertising on television."

"Won't you be back in Kissimmee in the fall, in school?"

Ted is at a loss for words, but only for a moment. "That remains to be seen," he says slowly. "Are you going back?"

"Why would I ever want to do that?" I ask.

## THIRTY-SEVEN

It's long after midnight. I am having trouble falling asleep. Then, somewhere between awake and dreaming, it hits me.

It's brilliant!

I'm brilliant!

I have finally figured out how to find Gunnar.

## ★ THIRTY-EIGHT ★

When I wake up I can't remember what my brilliant idea was. This is maddening. I sit and watch Twig drawing pictures on the ads in the newspaper and try to remember.

"Look at how funny this man looks," Twig says as she puts goggly eyes, long hair, and a dress on a man in a lab coat touting "Pain-free dentistry!"

That's when it hits me. "Thank you, Willow!" I shout. She looks confused, but I'm not. I remembered my brilliant idea.

Benito's Taco Truck #4 is early. I run toward it, but it looks like Jess has almost everything set up. She's already taking out the meats. I grab the Jarritos and start plunging them into the ice coolers built into the side of the truck.

As always, the time on the taco truck flies by. Jess says that the truck has been making more money since I started working there. Her Uncle Benny has noticed it too.

"So you've told him about me?"

"Not yet." Jess nibbles on a pickled carrot. "Uncle Benny has made it clear this is a family-run business. He'd consider you an outsider, plus you're not even Mexican. Anyway, he'd kill me for hiring you without his permission. It's still his name on the truck."

I feel kind of hurt that Jess won't tell Uncle Benny about me.

By two P.M., we've fed our last customer, and now my favorite time of day begins. Jess makes herself a pollo burrito with red rice and beans, cheese, lettuce, hot salsa with extra cilantro, and jalapeños on the side. Today I'll have three carnitas tacos in a corn tortilla with caramelized onions, sautéed mushrooms, and extra guacamole — always extra guacamole. We make it fresh every day using green scallions and ripe red tomatoes that Uncle Benny gets at the farmers' market. Jess had shown me how to mash it so that there are chunks of avocado in it. "None of that fake creamy stuff you get at the grocery store," she says. "This is authentic."

We both down a couple of ice-cold Jarritos. Bottled soda tastes a hundred times better than from a can. The sky is clear and it looks like there are flecks of gold in the ocean. "Jess," I begin. I've waited all day to tell her my news. "I've figured out how to find him."

"Who?"

"Gunnar, my father. I'm going to take out an ad, in the trades. That's what Hollywood calls the TV/movie papers. If my father is still in show business, he's sure to see it. Everyone in entertainment reads *Variety*."

I take out a piece of paper from my shorts pocket and show the ad to her. I created it on Sammy's computer.

Jess smiles. "Maybe, if that doesn't do it, I don't know what will."

## ★ THIRTY-NINE ★

**S**he what?"

"Chessy's joined Alcoholics Anonymous," Ridgeway says again. "It was her idea. Jake came on to one of her few remaining students. Chessy called him on it, kicked him out, and downed enough Jack Daniels to pickle her liver. Then she headed straight to AA. She'd been tipping back the bottle more than ever since you left, but this last Jake incident — well, even she recognized she's got a problem."

I let this sink in.

"Jake tried to rape someone else?"

"He says he was just fooling around, but the girl says otherwise. Her family might press charges."

"I hope they do," I mutter. "So does my mom believe me now? Does she see that he's a total asshole jerk?"

"She's not doing much talking these days, darling," Ridgeway informs me.

"Mostly she sits in your room and cries. But AA's been helping her a lot. And her sponsor is excellent. He's handsome too. She's probably going to want to marry the bastard."

"How do you know? I thought AA was supposed to be anonymous."

"I'm her sponsor."

"But don't you have to be a member to be a sponsor?" Then it dawns on me. "You're in AA? Ridgeway, you don't even drink."

"Not anymore. Maybe, do you want me to say anything to your mother for you? She's really hurting."

"I have nothing to say to her."

## ★ FORTY ★

We are sitting at Kozak's Koffee Shop, a place famous for having toasters on every table. Hollywood's just sent his documentary in to the contest, so the three of us are supposed to be celebrating, but I don't feel very festive. I can't get my mind off of that sleazebag Jake. He did it again. Only this time he got caught. Hollywood turns on his camera. "Maybe, any words about my documentary being finished?"

I bat the camera away. "Not now, Hollywood."

"Miss de la Tour was thrilled that her movie sold out," Ted says as he plays with the toaster.

I remove the butter knife from his hands. "You could get electrocuted," I scold him. "And the movie wasn't sold out. There was hardly anybody there."

"I told her it was packed," Ted says solemnly. "And I'm sure it would be, if it were promoted properly. By the way, she's fascinated with your search for your father. Miss de la Tour was an orphan too."

"I'm not an orphan."

I slump back in the booth. Suddenly I have a headache. It feels like a migraine or possibly a brain tumor, maybe both.

"Are you all right?" Hollywood puts his camera down just as two slices of toast pop up.

"She's probably had too much to eat," Ted says, feeling my forehead and then trying to look up my nose. "Maybe has a thing for carbs when she's on her period. Plus she gets super moody."

"Ted, can you shut up and take me home?"

"See what I mean?"

"I can take you home," Hollywood volunteers, already scooting out of the booth.

"If you insist," Ted agrees as another piece of toast pops up. He adds it to the two-story house of toast he's building.

"Are you okay?" Hollywood asks. His car backfires. Neither of us flinches, even though several people on the street duck for cover.

"Yeah," I say, rolling down the window. There's a definite difference between riding in a Rolls-Royce and the Green Hornet. "I just have a slight headache."

Hollywood turns on the radio. Some sappy station goes in and out as we head up the coast. He seems too preoccupied to notice. Before we get to Sammy's house, Hollywood pulls over on the side of the road. The only light is from the moon. I can hear the ocean crashing in the distance.

"Maybe?" Hollywood sounds nervous. "There's something I need to tell you."

Oh God. I just want to get home and go to bed. I can't believe Hollywood's picked now to talk. I know what he's going to say, and I've been dreading this conversation ever since he tried to kiss me last year. (We both pretended that nothing happened.)

"That's okay," I tell him. "You don't need to say anything."

"But I have to tell you, it's been eating me up inside."

"Really," I insist. God, he's making my headache worse. "Please don't say anything."

"But —"

"Hollywood, I know, okay." I've always suspected he's had a crush on me.

"You know? How do you know?"

"I just do." No point in embarrassing the poor guy. Plus, I don't need this right now.

"I thought I was pretty good at keeping it a secret," Hollywood stammers.

"It was fairly obvious."

"Yeah . . . it's not really something you can hide. Are you mad at me?"

I soften. He is so sweet. If only he weren't . . . so Hollywood.

"How could I be mad about that? I'm a little uncomfortable," I explain honestly. He's wearing that stupid lopsided grin. "But I'm flattered, and I value our *friendship*." I try to emphasize the word *friendship*. "And that's what I want, okay. For us to remain friends. Hollywood, can you do that?"

"Of course I can! I thought about not saying anything at all, but I'm glad I did. I mean, you'd eventually find out, right? I can't hide this from you forever."

Hollywood leans over to give me a kiss. I push him away.

"Whoa, back off, boy. *Friends*. Friends only, okay?"

He smiles sheepishly, then shakes my hand. I hope I haven't hurt him too much.

"Friends," he says. He almost looks relieved.

"Hollywood," I say softly. "Are you going to be all right?"

"I'm more than all right, Maybe. I'm thrilled that we had this talk and that you don't hate me."

He's so sweet. How could you hate someone for liking you?

## ★ FORTY-ONE ★

The lunch rush is over. I am stirring the refried beans as Jess counts how many tortillas are left. Her mother makes them daily by hand. Suddenly, Jess looks up and her eyes grow big. "Look at that!"

We get the occasional fancy sports car, but a Rolls-Royce is a Benito's first. "Those are my friends," I boast.

From a distance they look like an odd duo — too-tall Hollywood and tiny Ted. He's wearing his fedora, which makes him look more ridiculous than normal.

"So this is the famous Benito's Taco Truck #4," Ted booms as he approaches.

"What should we get?" asks Hollywood as he takes out his camera. "What's al pastor? Is it religious?"

"Hey guys," I say. "This is Jess, my boss."

She blushes and says, "I'm Maybe's friend."

"Jess, as in Jesse James?" Hollywood quips. It's a totally lame joke, but Jess laughs. I'm glad she's being nice to him. He's probably still devastated from last night.

"We're her friends too," Ted announces. "I'm Ted, that's Holly —"

"Hi, I'm Daniel," Hollywood says, reaching out to shake Jess's hand.

"This is on me, guys," I tell them. "Have a seat."

As Jess and I head into the truck, she whispers, "He's cute."

"Ted?"

"No, Daniel."

Hollywood cute? I take a second look. His acne seems to have cleared up and he's gotten some color, so he doesn't look quite as pasty as he used to.

Jess and I carry out an assortment of tacos. When Hollywood offers Jess his chair, Ted looks shocked. "When did you get manners?" he asks.

Hollywood ignores him. Instead, he fetches another chair and sits down next to Jess, leaving me standing. Ted eyes Jess as he digs into the tacos. "Wow, you're pretty and a good cook?" he crows with his mouth full. "I think I'm in love."

"This is the best taco I've ever tasted," Hollywood tells her.

Ted moves his chair between the two of them. "I can eat a lot," he informs Jess. "I think I'm going through a growth spurt."

The guys crowd around Jess. Anytime Hollywood starts to ask her something, Ted interrupts with his own lame question. I get up to get a soda.

"Hey waitress, get me another one, will you?" Ted calls out.

"Can I fetch anyone else anything?" I ask sarcastically.

They all call out their drink orders. Hollywood asks for more guacamole and then immediately turns his attention back to Jess. He certainly seems to have gotten over me fast.

When I'm in the truck, Jess rushes in all flushed. "Maybe, your friends are great, and good eaters too. I'm going to make some more tacos."

"They're okay," I say nonchalantly. "Holl — Daniel used to have really bad acne."

"Oh," Jess says, as the onions sizzle. "Well, you can't tell. It's gone now. And his hair. I've never seen hair like that. Don't you just want to pat him on the head?"

Nooooo, I want to punch him in the head sometimes. "You don't think his hair is weird?"

Jess laughs and gives me a sly look. "I like people with weird hair, Maybe."

As she grabs some extra napkins, Jess keeps chattering about Hollywood. It starts to bug me until I realize I should be happy that my friends are getting along. I try to chill out.

"Hey, I'll bet Ted will give you a ride in the Rolls if you ask him."

Jess's face lights up. "Really?"

"Sure!" I say a little too enthusiastically.

"Oh, wait." Jess shakes her head. "I can't leave the taco truck. If anything happens, Uncle Benny will kill me."

"I'll stay with the truck."

"Would you? Oh Maybe, you're the best!"

After Ted polishes off the rest of the tacos, there's a mad scramble to see who will open the car door for Jess. I'm kind of hoping Hollywood will offer to stay with me, but I'm left alone. As I wipe down the inside of the truck, I spot something on the floor near the driver's seat.

*Dear Ms. Jessica Consuelo Guadalupe Morales Lopez,*
*After careful review of your application and references, we are happy to offer you admission to Princeton University . . .*

It's dated several months ago. I slip it back in the envelope and put it on the dashboard just as the white Rolls-Royce pulls up next to the taco truck. Everyone inside is laughing as Jess gets out. "Thanks for the ride!"

There is a chorus of "Our pleasure," and "We should do this again," and "See you later, Jessica."

"Okay, Maybe," Ted shouts, "your turn. I'll drive you home."

Jess whispers to me, "Maybe, you are so lucky to have friends like that."

I smile weakly. "I guess I am."

As I get in the Rolls, Hollywood gets out. He shrugs. "Ted says he needs to talk to you alone first. I'll just wait with Jessica, I guess."

Is Ted trying to play matchmaker now?

I get into the front seat. Ted takes something out of his briefcase. "Thought you might want to see this. Check out page thirty-seven."

I gasp. There it is. My ticket to finding my biological father. I stare at the ad that Hollywood helped me write and that Ted placed in *Variety* for me. There's the picture of Gunnar, with Chessy cropped out, and below it reads:

*Desperately Seeking Gunnar!*
*Taken in Florida, November 1992*
*Gunnar, please call (407) 555-7132*
*or e-mail 911maybe@gmail.com*

My heart races. This has got to work. If it doesn't, I may as well give up.

## ★ FORTY-TWO ★

Jess is humming as she chops onions. I'm on the grill today. We work like a team that's been together for years. I can do everything she does, though not quite as well. Still, I've gotten good enough that when it's not too busy, Jess goes for a walk on the beach and leaves me alone to run Benito's Taco Truck #4. I've learned to banter with the men, laugh at the funny jokes, and shoot down the stray ones that are stupid or sexist or both.

"Are you okay?" Jess asks when she returns.

"Why do you ask?"

Jess shakes her head. "No reason, just wanting to make sure. You seem distant."

"It's been three days and he hasn't called."

"Who?"

"My father."

"Three days isn't a long time. Maybe he hasn't seen the ad yet."

"*Variety*'s a daily publication. So if he hasn't read it by now, he probably won't."

I don't want to talk about my search. Sometimes I'm sorry that I even mentioned him to Jess. She always wants to talk about what's going on and it's humiliating to never have any news. "What's up with you?"

"Well," Jess says, as she throws the onions into a plastic container. A shy smile crosses her face. "I have a date."

"You do? With who? Tell me!"

"Daniel."

I drop a tortilla on the floor. "My Daniel?"

"Is that a problem? I thought you guys were just friends."

"It's fine," I laugh, trying to sound lighthearted. "We are just friends. I mean, come on! Me and Daniel, that's funny." *When did he call her? They just met.* "Hey, it's great you guys are going out. He's great! Why should it be any of my business who either of you goes out with? You two will have a lot of fun!"

All the way home, I can't stop thinking about Jess and Hollywood dating.

Sammy and Willow are snacking on sushi when I get home. Vilma was here today so the house looks great and smells like lemons. Candles illuminate the table even though it's still afternoon. Willow is wearing a red kimono. I don't ask why.

"We got you a California roll," Sammy says. California rolls are my favorite. I love the avocado in them.

"Uh, no thanks, I'm not hungry."

As I head to my room I hear Willow say, "She's so strange."

Hollywood and Jess? Well, why not? He's free to go out with anyone he wants. And I did tell him that I just wanted to be friends.

Twig is still wearing the kimono when I surface at 9:30 P.M. in search of food. Sammy is already sleeping. It used to bug Chessy that he went to bed so early, and I can tell it bothers Twig too. I think she'd prefer going to clubs and parties than hanging around the house.

As Twig sashays around the living room she tilts her head to one side and says, "I like it!"

"You like what?" I grumble.

"Black beer soda. I got a part in a Japanese television commercial! Blondes are very popular in Japan."

She slumps across the room.

"I like it!

"I like it!

"I like it!"

I retreat to my room and pick up the phone.

"It's me."

"He hasn't called," Ted reports. I can hear him eating potato chips.

"He hasn't e-mailed me, either. But that's not why I'm calling. I have gossip."

"Let's hear it."

"Hollywood's going out with Jess."

"No way! Hollywood and Jess?"

"My thoughts exactly."

Ted releases a deep sigh. "Well, there goes a good one."

Just as I hang up the phone, Twig knocks on the door. "Maybe, is this a good time to talk?"

"No."

"Okay, good." She pushes the stuffed animals onto the floor and sits in the rocking chair. I consider kicking her out of my room, then remember that Twig has been semi-nice to me lately. "It's Sammy," she says.

"What about him?"

"I don't know where we're at. He doesn't say much and when I try to talk about us, he shuts down."

"That's just the way he is," I explain. "He's not a big talker."

"Well, I know he used to be married to your mom once . . ."

"Twice."

"Twice?"

I nod. This information leaves Twig momentarily speechless. Finally she says, "Okay, so then commitment is clearly not an issue with him. Maybe, why do you think he can't commit to me? He hasn't even, he hasn't said, he won't . . . never mind."

"He won't what?"

"I don't even know how he feels about me. Sometimes I think he just let me move in with him because he was lonely. He once told me that I reminded him of someone."

*Duh.* Had Twig not noticed the photos of Chessy that used to weigh down the walls? Could she not see the resemblance?

"I think I might lose the beer commercial," Twig sighs. She picks a plush poodle up off the floor and hugs it. "I really want this job to prove to Sammy that I'm worthy. But my agent says that I slouch, and if I slouch during the shoot, I'll be replaced."

I look up at her. She's on the verge of tears. "Willow, she's right," I say gently. "You do slouch."

"Well, your hair looks like hell," she yells, throwing the poodle in my face. "So don't go around thinking you're better than me. You're just a loser with bad hair!"

As I pick up the poodle, I think about Twig. She's not that bad. Not like the Fantastic Five. She's even tried to help me.

"Willow?" I call out as I walk through the house looking for her. "Willow?"

Twig is sitting on the front porch puffing on a cigarette. Some people look cool when they smoke. Twig looks stupid. "I don't slouch!" she insists. She tosses her cigarette onto the ground and stubs it out with the pointy toe of her shoes.

"Yes, you do," I tell her as she follows me into the house. "You walk like an old lady." I know I'm going to regret what I am about to say, but can't stop myself. "Willow, I can teach you how to stop slouching."

"You can? How?" Twig grabs my arm. "Oh please, please, please, Maybe," she begs, "help me!"

It's as if a lifetime of CC's Charm School training is coming back to me. I take a book off the shelf and put it on top of Twig's head.

"Walk," I command.

The book slips and hits the floor with a thud.

"Again, but this time throw your shoulders back, like this. And hold your head up high," I say. Then I add, channeling Chessy, "Pretend you have a neck brace on. 'Cause if you don't do this right, you'll be wearing one when I strangle you."

Fear flashes in Twig's eyes.

"Kidding," I tell her. "Willow, chill out, I'm only kidding!"

For the next few hours, I yell at Twig and she does what she's told. It is almost fun. Finally, when she's able to saunter across the room with a plate on her head and an egg on the plate, I know I have really accomplished something. Who knew telling someone to stand up straight could be so rewarding?

## ★ FORTY-THREE ★

**H**e is soooo sweet."

All Jess can talk about is Hollywood. I'm doing everything in my power not to puke. It would be bad for business. "He's kind of a dork, if you must know," I tell her as I pass an al pastor burrito, extra rice, extra cheese, no onions, over the counter.

"Where's the extra side of salsa?" the customer asks. I hand him a small plastic container, and he stares at me until I give him two more.

I turn back to Jess, who's now dicing more tomatoes. "I mean, Daniel's really nice and everything, but he's always got that awful Super 8 camera. It's kind of weird, don't you think?"

"What's carnitas?" the next customer asks. "What's the difference between that and al pastor?" We get this all the time. Dutifully, I recite the different kinds of tacos twice. He decides on beef taquitos.

"Daniel didn't bring the camera on our date," Jess says, picking up our conversation as I make change for a twenty.

"He didn't?" That's weird. I've never seen Hollywood without his camera. "So, uh, what did you guys talk about?"

Jess's eyes get all misty. I check to see if it's the onions, but they're nowhere near her. "Everything. It's so easy to talk to Danny. We talked about college, and our goals and dreams . . ."

*Danny?*

"Three pollo tacos," someone yells. "Hold the salsa, I'm allergic to tomatoes!"

Hollywood used to talk about his dreams with me. Not that I care. I don't have a monopoly on dreams. But he wouldn't have gotten into USC if I hadn't kept pressuring him to apply.

"Are you guys going out again?" I toss some marinated chicken on the grill and sprinkle it with salt and cayenne pepper. I feel a headache coming on. I must be dehydrated.

Jess nods. "Danny says we should all go out together. You know, him and me, and you and Ted."

"Wouldn't that cramp your date?"

"He didn't even kiss me good night," Jess confides. "Not yet, anyway."

I take a swig of soda. My headache seems to be going away.

After cleaning up around the taco truck, I hurry home. I've promised to help Willow with her posture again. She's waiting for me outside the house. "Look!" she says without even bothering to say hello. "I think I've got it!" I follow Willow into the house as she sashays like a model on the catwalk. No trace of slouching here. After more posture drills, I am confident that she's going to do all right. We both collapse onto the couch, laughing and congratulating ourselves. Sammy walks in and doesn't even try to hide the look of surprise on his face.

"Maybe was just helping me with my beer commercial," Willow explains gleefully.

"She's going to be great," I tell him.

"Oh, okay," Sammy says, still clearly stunned. "May I take you two out to dinner?"

"I'll grab my purse," Willow says. "Can we eat Japanese?"

Sammy turns to me. Even though he's always offered, I've never gone out with him and Willow before.

"I'll get my jacket."

At Tsujimoto's Sushi, Willow peels off the tempura batter and nibbles on a string bean.

"Just take a couple of bites," Sammy urges, holding out a shrimp with his chopsticks. "Look at Maybe, see how much she's eating."

That was probably the worst thing he could say. I know Willow thinks I eat too much.

"I'm not hungry," she whines.

"You're never hungry," Sammy groans. "Listen, you're beautiful, but if you don't gain some weight, you're going to get sick, and then your career will be over before it gets started."

Willow bites the string bean in half. Sammy turns to me. "So Maybe, how's Benito's Taco Truck #4?"

"It's doing great." I reach for my second piece of sashimi and dip it into the wasabi and soy sauce. "Hey, Sammy, could you do me a favor? I have some ideas to drum up more business."

Before I can tell him my plan, Willow holds up her glass. "I like it! I like it! I like it!"

"She's rehearsing," I explain to Sammy. "She shoots her beer commercial on Monday."

"Well, you'd better be sure to eat more before you drink," he warns her.

"I like it!" Willow says. "I like it!"

Sammy and I look at each other and break out laughing.

"What's so funny?" Willow asks. "Can someone tell me what's funny?"

## FORTY-FOUR

The only e-mails I've received from the ad are from people asking for money, people asking if I'm a movie producer, and people offering to find Gunnar if I pay them.

"Nope, nothing," Ted says when I call him. "Oh wait, there was one call." I perk up. "It was from *Variety*. They wanted to know if you want to run the ad again."

"Forget it," I say. I'm beginning to think that maybe Chessy made up the whole thing about my biological father. For all I know, he's some good ol' boy in Kissimmee.

"Miss de la Tour thinks you ought to try a psychic," Ted is saying. "I told her about Madame Poupon, but she says you should go to a real one. Not one at the mall."

"You tell her about me?"

"Of course. We can't talk about me all day."

"What else does the mighty Gloria de la Tour think about me?"

"She thinks that you're lucky to have me as a best friend. And she thinks that you should be nicer to Hollywood, and that you ought to be grateful to Sammy for taking you in, and that Jess has been good for you, and that you should call your mother —"

"Ted, what makes you think you can just tell a stranger all about my life?"

"One," he says, "Gloria de la Tour is not a stranger, she's my friend —"

"You can't be friends with your boss."

"You're friends with Jess."

"Yeah, okay. Wait. Hold on, Ted, I've got a call on the other line." I press the call-waiting button. "Hello?"

"Maybe?" It's Hollywood. His voice sounds weird, like he's been crying.

"Hollywood, is everything all right?"

"Yes, no, yes! It's more than all right. Maybe, I won! I won the student documentary contest!"

I break into a grin. "Oh, Hollywood, I am so happy for you!"

"You will be at the awards screening, right? Maybe, promise me you'll be there!"

"I promise, Hollywood. I promise."

"It's a miracle," he gushes. "A real miracle. I gotta call Jess now and tell her. Will you let Ted know?"

"Of course. Hollywood," I add, "I am so proud of you."

Ted is upset. "What is so important that you had to put me on hold for so long?" he demands.

"It was Hollywood on the other line."

"Did he ask about me?"

"Nooooo, but he did want me to tell you that he won the documentary competition!"

"I knew it!" Ted cries. "I always knew he had it in him. I'm going to call him right now."

"He's talking to Jess. Maybe you should wait a bit."

"Are Jess and Hollywood, like, an official item?"

"It's starting to look like it."

"Oh. I see," he answers. "I'll talk to you later. I promised Maah and Paww I'd call them."

As I clean my room I think about Hollywood. At least someone's realizing their dream.

The canopy is off my bed. The frilly bedspread is gone too. In its place is a patchwork quilt I got at the thrift store. A Benito's T-shirt is tacked up on the wall next to the *Nelson's Neighborhood* poster with Christian Culver giving a thumbs-up. The photo of me and Chessy and Sammy is still on the dresser. I wonder what she's doing tonight.

I open the closet. Inside is the big photo of Chessy wearing her bathrobe. I found it in the garage with the other pictures. "Why are you so difficult?" I say out loud.

When no one answers, I put the photo back and close the closet door.

## ★ FORTY-FIVE ★

We're at dinner. Pizza. Ever since Hollywood won the student film competition last week, he's turned into Mr. Chatterbox.

"They've rented a theater in Beverly Hills. Beverly Hills! I'm going to be making my big-screen debut!"

"You're going to need a manager," Ted proclaims. Like a magician he makes a business card materialize and hands it to Hollywood.

Hollywood bursts out laughing. "Since when did you become a manager?"

"Let me see that!" I grab the card. Sure enough, gold letters spell out Ted's name, Miss de la Tour's address, and the words MANAGER TO TOP TALENT.

"I can rep you too, Maybe."

"I don't have a talent. That's why I was never good at charm school, a beauty pageant queen, or a credit to my mother."

"Not true," Ted frowns. "It wasn't just because you didn't have a talent. There were lots of other reason why you weren't crown-worthy."

I throw a pizza crust at him. "Shut up, cockroach!"

Undeterred, Ted turns to Hollywood. "Daniel, let's discuss your career."

"I thought you worked for Gloria de la Tour," Jess says. She's usually quiet when all of us are together. I think she's a little unnerved because Ted and I fight so much. Plus, there's that whole Hollywood/Jess thing going on.

"I do work for Miss de la Tour," Ted explains as he helps Jess eat her fries. "But even though she's promoted me from Executive Assistant to Manager, she doesn't have an exclusive."

"Miss de la Tour doesn't mind that you want to represent other people too?" asks Hollywood. He starts eating off of Jess's plate.

"She's not aware of that yet. But she'll be fine with it. Whatever Teddy wants, Teddy gets."

I roll my eyes. "You are so full of yourself!"

We shove each other until Jess speaks up. "Ahem, let's talk about Danny's screening, okay?"

Hollywood blushes. She blushes too. It's so corny.

"Well, we have to get there early," he explains. "We'll have reserved seats near the front —"

"Excuse me," Ted interrupts, "when you say *we*, who exactly do you mean?"

"All of us," Hollywood says, gesturing around the table.

Ted waves him on. "Continue."

"They'll show the finalists' films first. Then someone from First Take — those are the people who sponsored the contest — will give a speech and they'll show the grand prize film — that would be mine." Hollywood pauses. "I just wish my family could be here."

"I'm going to be there, big guy." Ted slaps him on the back.

"Me too," Jess adds.

"That's nice," Ted says, pushing her plate of fries away. "But I've known him for years. I knew him when he was just a geek with a small camera and a big dream." He turns to Hollywood. "Don't you worry, I'll make sure you don't sign anything you shouldn't. By the way, what's the film about? The theme? The plot? The denouement?"

"Yeah, tell us," I urge.

"It's a big secret," Jess says. "Danny won't even tell me."

I glance at Hollywood and he winks. Quickly, I turn away. Did I just see that? He's flirting with me with Jess right here?

I look back at him and he gives me a little smile.

He *is* flirting with me! After our I-want-to-be-friends talk.

"C'mon, Ted, I gotta go," I say. "I promised Willow I'd teach her how to enunciate."

"But I want to stay," Ted whines.

"Let's go," I order.

Ted looks mournfully at Hollywood and Jess. "Can we trust these two alone together?"

Both laugh nervously. I wave good-bye, and when I look at Hollywood, he winks again.

What's with that?

## ✦ FORTY-SIX ✦

**S**ammy pulls his BMW up next to the taco truck. Willow is with him. Ever since I gave her posture lessons, she's been acting like my new best friend. I think I liked it better when we despised each other.

"Wow," Willow says, as she gets out of the car. She's wearing a short skirt and high heels. "This is so cute. It's like a little restaurant on wheels!" Some of the construction workers whistle and Willow waves at them.

"What's going on?" Jess asks as Sammy gets his equipment out of his car.

"That's Sammy, my ex-stepdad. He's going to take photos of the food. That way people can just point to the pictures instead of us having to explain what everything is."

Jess pulls me aside. "Maybe, I can't afford photos!" She sounds panicked. "You should have asked me first."

"This isn't going to cost you anything, Sammy's doing it for free."

"Why would he do that for me?" The steak on the grill is burning as Jess keeps a wary eye on Sammy.

"He's not doing it for you," I assure Jess. "He's doing it for me."

The rest of the afternoon, Jess and I cook up every item on the menu. I had no idea photographing food could be so intense. Sammy scrutinizes each plate we bring out, sometimes asking us to prepare another one if it doesn't look perfect. When he takes the photos, Jess stands back, biting her fingernails, until Sammy says, "Okay, got it!"

As the afternoon wears on, Jess begins to enjoy herself. "How's this?" she asks, carrying out five plates of tacos.

"Gorgeous," Sammy tells her. Jess can't hide her smile. "Not only do they look great, they smell great."

"Taste one," Jess says.

Sammy lifts up an al pastor taco. Jess hands him some guacamole. We hold our breath as he bites into it. When he breaks into a contented grin, Jess and I exhale. "My God, Jess," Sammy says as he reaches for his second one, "I'm in taco heaven!"

Jess glows.

Willow, clearly bored, watches the construction workers watch her.

After the last taco is photographed, Sammy tells Jess, "I'm just going to take some candids of you and Maybe working in the truck. It's for my portfolio. I'll make sure to get you copies."

Jess and I look at each other. We're both sweaty, our hair is a mess, and we have food all over our Benito's T-shirts. As if reading our minds, Sammy says, "These are just candids, it's not a fashion shoot."

"I guess it's okay." Jess shrugs.

It seems like only a few seconds have gone by when Sammy has Jess laughing and talking while he takes the pictures. He even gets in the truck and has Willow stand in line like she's a customer. This is actually fun.

I hand Willow a taco. "Here, try this."

She recoils like it's poison. "I'm not hungry."

"It won't kill you."

"Take a bite for the camera," Sammy orders.

She nibbles and makes a face. Her body probably isn't used to real food.

Before he leaves, Sammy orders a half dozen tacos to go. Jess refuses to take his money. She includes a big container of her famous salsa in his bag. Later, as I Windex the windows and Jess scrapes the grill, she says, "Man, Maybe, your dad is so cool."

"Ex-stepdad . . ." I start to correct her, but instead I just say, "Yeah, I'm pretty lucky."

When I get home, Sammy's on the patio talking on the phone. He's very animated. Willow is sitting on the couch, hugging her skinny knees.

"Hey Willow —"

"Shhhh, he's talking to someone."

"I can see that —"

"Shhhhh!"

"Yes, well, I thought so too." With the waves crashing behind him, it's hard to hear. "Well," he laughs, "you didn't look so bad yourself that day . . . yes, hmmm . . . I think about you too . . ."

Willow gets up and goes into the kitchen. I follow her. She opens the bag of tacos and starts eating. "What?" she protests with her mouth full. "Haven't you ever seen anyone eat before?"

"I've never seen *you* eat before."

She glares at me but doesn't stop.

"Slow down. You'll make yourself sick."

Willow starts to cry. "What'll I do? What'll I do if he leaves me?"

"He's not going to leave you. He's just talking on the phone."

"Yeah, but his cell phone rings late at night sometimes, and even if he's asleep he gets up to answer it and goes into the bathroom to talk."

I take the taco from her hands and put it on the counter, far from her reach. "I'm sure it's no big deal."

"Really?"

"Really."

Willow thinks her life will end without Sammy. How can I tell her that people come and go all the time, and after a while you just get used to it?

"The trick is to leave them before they leave you," Chessy once told me. "Don't ever let them get too close. That way they can't hurt you."

I can't say she didn't teach me anything.

## ★ FORTY-SEVEN ★

**N**ow that Willow's mentioned it, I do notice Sammy on his cell phone a lot. When he catches me looking at him, he leaves the room. Willow has gone from no eating to nonstop eating.

"Hey," I say. She's staring at an empty bag of Milanos as if willing more to magically appear. "I have to go to Hollywood's documentary screening in a couple days and I don't have anything to wear."

Her eyes get big. "I can help you with that."

"That would be nice."

"I can do your makeup and hair too," she offers, smiling for the first time in days.

I want to laugh because her brown roots are showing and she looks awful. Instead I say, "Well, if you just help me with the clothes, that would be enough."

Willow tosses the Milanos bag and rises from the couch. "Okay then, come on."

We are in her massive closet. It seems even more packed than last time. She pairs a plain navy blue T-shirt with a green silk jacket. "This should fit you — it's way too big for me. And these will go with your jeans," Willow says. She adds gold earrings and a chunky gold necklace, and those wobbly black boots again.

"This is what I'm wearing," Willow announces. She pulls out a slinky silver dress and killer stiletto heels.

"You're going too?"

"Daniel invited me and Sammy. I figured there might be movie people there, so we should go."

I don't know why I am surprised. It's only natural that Hollywood would want people he knows there to support him. He's still torn up because his family can't make it for his big night. I think he's a little homesick. Ted too.

Ted picks me up for a late dinner. Gloria de la Tour goes to bed at 8:30 P.M., so we mostly see each other in the evenings. All the way to Pink's Hot Dogs in Hollywood, he jabbers nonstop to his parents. "I know, I know, Maah, I miss you too," he's saying. When he lowers his voice, I try not to listen. Still, I can tell he's about to cry.

By the time we get to Pink's, Ted has Yo-Yo Ma blasting on the stereo and is back to his chipper self, or at least pretending to be. As usual, all the tables are full so we sit on the curb. I've ordered one of Pink's famous chili dogs. Ted has a plain hot dog with extra relish. We share onion rings. I take my first bite of hot dog and savor the crunch. I swear, the hot dog pops when you bite into it. As I reach for an onion ring, Ted says casually, "Hey Maybe, your dad called."

"Sammy?"

"Your biological father."

I stop chewing and stare at Ted. "What did you just say?"

"Your father called. He left a message on my cell phone." Ted takes a U-No bar wrapper out of his pocket. "Here's his number."

"Why didn't you tell me earlier?" I shout, grabbing the wrapper. It's hard to read. Ted has horrible handwriting.

"I was talking to Maah and Paww, then I had to decide what hot dog to get. You know I have trouble deciding."

I stare at the phone number. I am seven digits away from my real father. My heart is racing. I get up and start to pace. This is it. This is it. This is it. I walk back and forth behind Ted until I start to wheeze. "Ted . . ." Still eating, he lifts his cell phone up high in the air. I take it from him and dial.

"Gary Germain Productions." It's a woman.

"Uh, hi," my voice cracks. "I'm calling for Gunnar."

"There's no Gunnar here."

"Are you sure?"

"Hon, I'm sure."

The phone goes dead.

I hang up and swat Ted. His hot dog hits the ground. "I thought you said my father called!"

"He did," Ted grumbles as he brushes off his hot dog. "He said he was your father and left this number."

Ted hits message playback. I listen to a man say, "Hey, I saw your ad in *Variety* and I think I may have some information about the person you're looking for. Call me."

"He didn't say he was my father," I yell. "He said he may have some information about the person I'm looking for. The lady at the number had no idea what I was talking about. It was probably a crank call."

Great. Now I'm crying. It's one thing for my mother to make me cry. But my father? I don't even know him and he's killing me.

All the way home, Ted's blathering about hot dogs and poly-cotton blends and Hollywood's hair is just background sound as I replay the lady saying, "There's no Gunnar here."

When Ted drops me off, he leans out the car window and says, "Hey, Maybe?"

"Yeah?"

"I'm sorry it wasn't him."

"Me too."

The next morning my eyes fly open and I bolt straight up in bed, thinking I'm late for school and that Chessy is going to yell at me. The sound of the waves reminds me that I am not in Kissimmee, I'm in Malibu, in Sammy's house, far away from school and my mother.

I stare at the number on the U-No bar wrapper. I pick up the phone and call again. This time a recording comes on. It's a man's voice. "You've reached Gary Germain Productions. Leave a message at the beep."

"Hi, this might sound weird," I say in a rush. "But did you once know someone named Chessy Chestnut from Kissimmee, Florida? Or maybe you know someone who did know her? My name is Maybelline and I've got some important news for Gunnar. I think he may be my father. Please call me back at (407) 555-7132."

I hang up and dial another number. It rings several times. "Hello?"

"Hi, it's me."

"Maybe, what time is it?"

I glance at the clock. Oh. "Um, it's six-thirty A.M."

"This better be good."

"Ted, I just wanted to tell you that I left a message at that man's number. Maybe he knows Gunnar and that's why he called. I left your number, so if he calls, I want you to set up a meeting for us."

"It's six-thirty A.M.?"

"Ted, I know and I'm sorry. But promise me you'll set up a meeting for us, okay? I can't give him Sammy's number. I don't want Sammy knowing what I'm up to."

"It's six-thirty A.M.!"

The phone goes dead. I hope Ted paid attention to what I was saying.

I have trouble going back to sleep, so I wander upstairs. Sammy is already up and reading the paper. He's a morning person. Willow sleeps until noon.

"Good morning, Maybe. Jess's photos came out great." Sammy doesn't seem fazed that I am up so early.

The proofs are spread all over the kitchen counter. Sammy is right — they do look terrific. I pause at a photo of a pretty girl laughing. Is that me? It doesn't look like me. She's barefaced and tanned. She looks happy.

"Sammy, these are amazing." He smiles. "I'm going to get the food shots mounted and laminated. That way Jess can put them up on the truck."

Sammy chuckles. "You're like your mom, Maybe."

"What do you mean?"

"Your ideas, they're great. Your mother has a head for business too. Remember all those ads she ran and how she insisted . . ."

" 'If you want them to take notice, take out an ad,' " we say in unison.

Then it hits me. It wasn't my idea to take out an ad in *Variety*. It was my mother's.

## ★ FORTY-EIGHT ★

Jess is Hollywood's date tonight and has talked of nothing else all day.

"Danny is so amazing."

"Danny is so talented."

"Danny is so smart."

Danny is getting on my nerves. I'm glad when work is over. There aren't many places you can hide in a taco truck.

When I get home, Willow is in her silver dress, strutting around with a plate on her head and an egg on the plate, and still she looks drop-dead gorgeous. Sammy looks nice too. He's wearing a suit and it reminds me of when he got married to my mother the second time.

"Hurry up, Maybe," Sammy says as he fixes his tie. "We don't want to be late!"

I shower and change into the outfit Willow and I picked out. She helps me with my makeup and hair, then stands back and looks me over. I return her smile.

There's not a lot of room in the BMW, so I'm squished in the backseat. I would love to put the top down, but Willow doesn't ant the wind to mess up her hair. She's done it up so it looks like there are little cinnamon buns stuck all over her head.

Even though we get to the theater early, the parking lot is crowded. A lot of the cars look expensive. I spot the Green Hornet with the tape on the left headlight and the photo of James Dean stapled to the dashboard. I don't see a white Rolls-Royce.

As soon as we walk into the building I spot Hollywood pacing in the lobby. He lights up and gives me a huge hug. I feel myself turning red when I see Jess standing behind Hollywood. As she steps in front of him I gasp. Jess is wearing a short red dress. She's got heels on. Her hair is curled and she's wearing lipstick. Jess looks beautiful.

"Excuse us, Jessica." Hollywood leaves Jess with Sammy and Willow and pulls me aside. He is wearing his sports jacket and he's done something to his hair. He actually looks good and smells good too. What's happening to everyone?

"Can you believe this?" Hollywood whispers. "Did you see the marquee? My name was up there! The head of the USC cinema department is here. My screenwriting professor is here. *You're* here!"

"This is so great, Hollywood. You deserve everything that's coming your way tonight." Just seeing how happy he is makes me want to cry. He's come so far from Kissimmee, where kids called him Hollyweird.

"Maybe, I can only tell this to you, but if I do ever make it big, do you know what I'm going to do first?" I shake my head. "I'm going to buy my mom a big house. No more trailer park for her!"

My eyes fill with tears. "It's going to happen someday, Hollywood. I just know it."

He hugs me and whispers, "This is our night, Maybe. Of all the people in the world, you're the one I want to share it with."

Uh-oh. He's starting that again, and with Jess standing just a few feet away. "Slow down, cowboy," I tell him, breaking away from his embrace. "It isn't our night, it's all yours."

"I couldn't have done it without you," he says, choking up. "I hope you like my film."

"Of course I'm going to like it, Hollywood. I trust you. I know that whatever you do is going to be great."

He smiles and whispers, "You're my inspiration."

I allow myself a smile. Even though I don't want him to get the wrong impression about our relationship, it's nice to be someone's inspiration.

A booming voice interrupts us. "Well, if it isn't Mr. Award-Winning Documentary Director!"

An obscenely large bouquet of flowers lumbers toward us. Behind it is Ted. He hands them to Hollywood. Rats. I should have brought something to give to him. Hollywood takes out a rose and presents it to Jess. She lifts it to her nose and smiles shyly. Then he hands me the rest of the flowers.

"For you," he says, winking.

I shove them back at him. "What are you doing?" I hiss.

"I had Ted pick these up for me," he says, looking hurt. "Don't you like them?"

Before I can say anything, the doors open into the theater and the crowd sweeps us inside. "Come on," Ted shouts. "Make way, make way," he cries as he passes out business cards. "We're with the winner here!"

We take our seats and I shift the flowers in my arms. The bouquet is too big to put on the floor. Some old-fart director gets up and gives a long-winded speech proclaiming, "The future of documentaries is in the room with us tonight." I sneak a glance at Hollywood. He's sitting ramrod straight as he listens, mesmerized by the old guy's blabbering.

Ted leans over and whispers, "He called. He's going to meet you here after the screening."

"Who?"

"That man who called about the ad."

"He's here?" I squawk.

Just then the lights dim and the curtains part.

"Quiet!" someone yells.

I can barely breathe. There are so many questions I want to ask Ted, but every time I open my mouth someone shushes me.

Each film is about fifteen minutes long. I'm sure they're good, but I'm having trouble focusing. I may find out about my father tonight. I am so close. What if that man's waiting in the lobby right now? What if he's sitting in the audience? What if he's my father? At the very least, he must be somehow connected to my father. I look around, but it's impossible to see anything. I try to breathe normally but end up hyperventilating. Ted keeps nudging me. "Knock it off," he whispers.

From what I can tell, the film that's on-screen is about a one-armed baton twirler. When she finds out she gets to march in the Rose Parade, several people in the audience begin to sob, including Ted.

*Hurry up and be over.*

*Hurry up!*

*Hurry up!*

The lights go back on and the old fart appears again. Ted yanks me back into my seat. I can't sit still.

"Tonight's grand prize for best student documentary was not a hard decision. Even though the competition was fierce, this young man's film grabbed the judges and wouldn't let go. He is someone whose name you should commit to memory. After the film, our winning director, Daniel Jones, will come up to say a few words. But now, sit back and enjoy the debut of a stunning new talent."

There is applause as the theater goes dark. I am so excited I can barely breathe. Not only is this Hollywood's big night, but my search is finally paying off. Ted and I hold hands. "Pretty soon, Maybe," he whispers.

On the huge screen, a bus drives up and the wheels grind to a stop. The door opens. Kids' feet flood the screen as they rush to class, chatting, yelling, laughing. The title comes up: *Absolutely Maybe.*

Suddenly, the buses drive away and we see a lone figure walking toward school. Ted squeezes my hand hard.

It's me!

It's me?

What am I doing there? The bell rings and the on-screen me doesn't even make any effort to hurry. If anything I slow down. The voice-over begins: "For Maybelline, also known as Maybe, school is just one more battle she must endure to get on with her life . . ."

Ted and I turn to each other. Both our jaws drop. Slowly we face the screen.

Hollywood shows me after I was beat up by Chessy's Charmers.

He shows me running last around the track in P.E.

He shows me being made fun of and laughed at.

He shows me crying after a fight with Chessy. "I don't know," the camera catches me confiding to Ted. "I sometimes wonder if it would have been better if I'd never been born."

It gets worse. Hollywood has one part where he shows a series of shots of me with different hair colors and messy haircuts. The voice-over says, "Even her hair doesn't know what it wants to be."

I feel like throwing up. I struggle to stand, but the flowers get in the way, so I hurl them across the dark auditorium. Someone yells, "Hey!"

"Shove it!" I yell as I make my way down the row, stepping on feet as I go. I race through the lobby, then out the front doors. When I get outside, I gasp for air, taking big gulps, like I'm drowning. Then I run and run, pushing people out of my way. I don't know where I am going. I don't know where I am. I'm lost. I'm lost. I'm lost, but I keep running.

I finally stop on Rodeo Drive. Everything looks bright and shiny, even the people. They are milling about, window-shopping, laughing, talking, oblivious that my miserable pathetic life is being splashed across the big screen at this very moment. What if my father was sitting in the audience? What if he saw what a loser I am? He'll never want to meet me now. This whole trip has been for nothing. My whole life has been nothing.

I hate Hollywood. If only he were here now, I'd show him how

I feel about his stupid documentary. I spot a tall potted palm tree and whack it. It doesn't hit back. It doesn't even move. So I begin to kick it and beat it with my fists. Someone is screaming and won't stop. A couple of policemen grab me. The screaming continues.

"Calm down, calm down," one of the cops says.

"Is she on drugs?" the other one asks. "Should I call for backup?"

"No, I think she's just flipped out."

"Leave me alone!" I realize the screaming has been coming from me. I break loose and attack the palm tree all over again.

The officers stand back and watch. The first one says, "Let us know when you're through destroying public property."

I kick the tree. I hit it. I push it. When I have nothing left, I slide down and sit at the base of the pot. A crowd has gathered. A couple of tourists take photos.

"What are you staring at?" I snap.

"How old are you?" the bigger cop asks. He looks like a movie star. When I don't answer, he repeats his question.

The other one, who is shorter and beefier, says, "We can do this the easy way or the hard way. The choice is yours. We'll need to see some ID."

I stare at the sidewalk. The beefy officer sighs. "Okay, miss. You want to do this the hard way, then. Please stand. I'm going to have to ask you to come with us."

## ★ FORTY-NINE ★

According to the poster on the wall, the mission of the Beverly Hills Police Department is to "provide superior law enforcement service, while making our community the safest place for all people to live, work, and visit."

I read it as I wait to get fingerprinted or whatever they do before they send me to prison to rot and die. On the booking sheet or whatever it's called, where it says "hair color," the cop had to write "green." The matronly-looking lady in front of me was arrested for DUI. She is still weaving as she grips the counter. I watch her pearl necklace sway back and forth, back and forth.

"Maybe?"

I turn around. It's Sammy. I don't know whether to cry and be angry, or cry and be happy, or cry and be relieved. So I just cry.

He gets on his cell phone. "I've got her, she's fine." Then he hugs me. "It's okay, it's okay." Sammy asks the beefy officer, "What did she do?"

"She assaulted a potted plant," he says, trying not to crack up. "Do you know this young lady?"

"She's my daughter." The cop's eyes go from him to me. "My stepdaughter."

"Okay, sir, I'm going to release her into your custody. Just make sure she gets some anger management therapy, or takes yoga, or something."

Sammy keeps a firm hand on my shoulder as he leads me toward the door. Once we're outside, he makes another call. "We're at the police station. Yeah. She's fine. Okay."

Willow is leaning against the BMW. She straightens up when she sees me. "Here," she says. "I gathered some of the flowers you dropped."

I didn't drop them, I threw them, but I just say, "Thanks, Willow."

"You really had us worried," Sammy says as he makes a slow left turn out of the police-department parking lot. "Want to talk about what happened?"

"No."

"Okay. Maybe later."

"Do you mind if we drive with the top down?" I ask. Sammy looks at Willow. She nods. He presses a button and the roof disappears.

Sammy plays a piece of classical music to mask our silence. Willow's cinnamon buns are coming loose. Finally, she lets them all out and her hair whips in the air. A sliver of moon slices through the water. My mind replays the scene of Chessy saying, "She's just the light of my life. A girl like her makes me feel proud of who I am — what? Who? Maybelline? No, no, no." My mother laughs. "I thought you were asking about Camilla, my latest pageant winner."

There are two cars parked in front of Sammy's house, a white Rolls-Royce and the Green Hornet. I don't want to go inside, but Sammy and Willow each take one of my arms. I am too tired to fight.

Hollywood and Ted are huddled at the dining-room table. Jess is on the patio. Sammy and Willow block the doorway. There is nowhere I can run.

"Maybe, I can explain," Hollywood says. He looks like he's in severe pain. "I thought you knew. We discussed this. That night when I tried to tell you about the documentary, you said you already knew and that no matter what we'd always be friends." His voice cracks. "You didn't even wait to see the end of the film."

"I saw all I needed to see," I say flatly.

"But you only saw the beginning —"

"I saw enough! I saw that you just used me all this time for your stupid film. Did you even consider how I might feel being up there? Oh, but wait. 'Director Daniel Jones, we expect great things from you.' So if you need to abuse your friends to get ahead, you just do whatever you need to do and don't worry about *me,* your pathetic slacker pal from Kissimmee."

"Maybe," he pleads, "I never would have done this if I thought it would hurt you."

I look into Hollywood's eyes. They are welling up with tears. One runs down his cheek, but he doesn't bother to brush it away. There is a knot in my throat. I open my mouth to say something, but instead I take a deep breath. He looks hopeful.

I sigh and shake my head. "I'm sorry," I whisper.

Then I gather all my strength and punch Hollywood in the face.

## ★ FIFTY ★

"N ot even her hair knows what it wants to be" keeps echoing in my head.

Slowly, I pick up the scissors and raise them high. Tufts of green hair float down and fill the sink as I cut and cut and cut. The more I cut, the worse I look. But I don't care. It's not like I'm entering a beauty pageant anytime soon.

★ ★ ★

Willow is devouring another taco. She looks good with the weight she's put on. "You shouldn't have hacked off your hair," Willow says, shaking her head. "It was sorry enough the way it was."

"It was a spur-of-the-moment inspiration."

"It looks like a really bad lawn," Willow tells me as she scrutinizes my head. "There's still some green poking through, but there are big empty patches like dirt, and then over there —"

"I get it, okay? Can you please shut up?"

Willow huffs and unwraps another taco. "You should watch Hollywood's film," she says as she licks her fingers. "I liked it."

"I don't want to watch it, or talk about it, or even think about it, okay?"

"Suit yourself." Willow turns her attention to her taco and smothers it with salsa.

I haven't gone to work for four days. I can't bring myself to face Jess. She's seen the documentary. She must know how worthless I am. Still, Jess delivers tacos every day on her way home. She just leaves the bag by the door.

Hollywood calls, but I just hang up. I don't bother opening his e-mails either. I talk to Ted twelve times a day on the phone, but I don't say anything, and I'm not sure if he even notices. He just blabs about Miss de la Tour, and his parents, and the price of homemade pasta. This morning he left a DVD of Hollywood's film in the mailbox, along with a teddy bear and a box of chocolates. They were all melted, but that didn't stop Willow from eating them.

## ★ FIFTY-ONE ★

**M**e awake! Me awake!"

Todd is clutching the bars of his crib, screaming. I am babysitting for Tessa and the triplets again. Even though Tammy, Todd, Tina, and I all ended up crying yesterday, Tessa wants me back on a regular schedule. She's even offered me more money. I told her I'd think about it.

As I trudge home I spot the Rolls-Royce in the driveway. Ted is jumping around on the front porch. His face is pinched and red. He's talking on his phone. "Yeah, she's finally here. Okay, gotta go. Love you, Maah!" Ted turns to me and growls, "It's about time you got here. I have to go to the bathroom. I almost peed in my pants." He gawks at my head. "What's with your hair? It looks seriously ugly."

"Please!" I moan. Still, I can't help but smile. Even a few days away from Ted is too many. Having used the bathroom, Ted's in a much better mood. He's at the table, swinging his feet, eating the leftover pad Thai that Sammy brought home for dinner last night. He's wearing Willow's faux fur. He just loves going through her closet when she's not home.

"No one makes Thai food as good as Maah," Ted tells me

through a mouthful of noodles. "Chef's cooking can't even compare to hers. And you should see the way Miss de la Tour's housekeeper irons. Maah could iron better blindfolded and with one hand tied behind her back.

"Hey, could you turn on the air-conditioning? It's hot in here." When I come back, Ted's on the phone again. "Don't cry. I miss you too . . . I know, I know. Well, Maah can sleep in my room if that'll make her feel better. Oh, Maybe's back. Gotta go, Paww."

Ted shuts his phone. "My parents aren't doing so well," he says, looking sad.

"Is anything wrong?"

"Of course something's wrong. Their beloved Teddy is not with them and they miss him." Ted sighs and shakes his head. "Hey, Maybe, you really freaked us all out when you ran out of the auditorium screaming."

"I was screaming?"

"It sure as hell wasn't me." Ted takes a long drink of water, then motions for me to refill the glass. "Hollywood got a standing ovation for his film. You should have stayed for the whole thing."

"I thought you were supposed to be my friend."

"I am your friend, that's why I put up with you. Hey, have you watched the DVD yet?" I shake my head. "Well, it's excellent, and I'm not just saying that because Hollywood is my biggest client, after Gloria de la Tour. The only change I would make to the film is to have more of me. You know, play up that good-looking best friend angle."

"Whose side are you on?"

"This is not a war."

"Yes it is. Hollywood made fun of me in front of the whole world. I looked like an idiot."

"You are an idiot. Watch the DVD. What is wrong with you? By the way," Ted says as he puts more pad Thai on his plate, "that guy called again."

"My father?"

"He didn't say. He just left a message saying his name was Gary Germain and he wanted to meet you. Here." Ted hands me a piece of paper.

"Tomorrow at noon at The Ivy," I read. I'm trembling. "Ted, I'm going to need a ride. Can you pick me up around eleven?"

"I have to work. Miss de la Tour is getting a new fountain and has entrusted me to see that it gets installed properly."

"Ted, this is important."

"Fountains are important to Miss de la Tour. Why don't you ask Hollywood or Sammy?"

"I'm not speaking to Hollywood, and Sammy doesn't know about this, remember?"

"What about Jess?"

"Right, like she's never busy at lunchtime. Just forget it," I mutter. "If you no longer want to be my best friend, just say so."

"Okay," Ted says. I'm speechless. I can't believe he's abandoning me. "Okay," he repeats. "OKAY, I'll do it."

"You will?" I squeal. He fights me off as I try to kiss him.

## ✳ FIFTY-TWO ✳

I'm obsessed with meeting this Gary Germain. It's all I can think about. Gunnar probably saw the documentary and decided to send Gary to check me out. I can't say that I blame him. I looked like such a loser. Now I've got to make a good impression on Gary so he can report back that I'm a person worth getting to know.

I dress in my jeans, a tank top, and one of Willow's jackets. As promised, Ted shows up precisely at eleven A.M., just as I am tying my Andy Warhol scarf around my head.

The drive to The Ivy seems longer than it took to get Los Angeles from Kissimmee. Ted talks to his mother on the phone during the entire drive. That's fine with me since I am so busy being nervous. "Good luck, Maybe," Ted says when we finally arrive.

I take his hand and squeeze it. "Thanks, Ted. See you in two hours."

My heart is beating so fast I'm afraid it'll knock me over. The restaurant is full of celebrities. I feel like I'm in the middle of one of Chessy's *Movie Maven* magazines. In the corner is Elizabeth Parisi — she's one of my mother's favorite soap opera stars. Three of the five members of Top Dog are sitting in the patio. Bennett

Slade, from the spy series, is at the bar. I'm not even sure who I'm looking for. Suddenly, a familiar-looking person walks in. I gasp. I would recognize him anywhere.

"Name?" the hostess asks.

"Christian Culver."

It's him! It's him! Nelson B. Nelson from *Nelson's Neighborhood*! He looks older, but of course he would. And he looks totally hot, more muscular, taller, tanner. Did he dye his hair blond?

"I'm sorry," the hostess says. "You're not on the list."

He leans in toward her and flashes her that winning Nelson B. Nelson smile — the one that made mean teachers and mad dogs melt. "I'm on a hit television series," he coos.

"Were." Her voice is icy. "You *were* on a hit television series. But you're not on the list today."

"I'm sure you have something . . ."

"You're not on the list," she repeats firmly. Her lips are pursed into a tight smile. You can tell she's enjoying this. His shoulders slump when he turns away.

I summon up my courage and approach him. "Nelson, er, Christian, I just wanted to say . . . uh, I wanted to say . . ."

"What?" he says sharply. "Spit it out."

". . . that I'm a huge fan."

"Tell it to her," he says bitterly.

The hostess notices me for the first time. She eyes me suspiciously, like I'm from another planet. Maybe I am.

"Name?"

"Maybelline Chestnut," I mumble as I watch Nelson B. Nelson walk out of the restaurant.

"You're not on the list," the hostess says as she smirks at my scarf.

"She's with me." A man steps up behind me. He's big and solid, like someone who used to be an athlete. His hair is short and dark, and he's wearing an expensive-looking Hawaiian shirt tucked into black jeans. "Maybelline?" he says, not bothering to remove his sunglasses.

"Mr. Germain?" I croak.

"Call me Gary. Rachel, honey, is my table ready?"

"Follow me, Mr. Germain!" Rachel smiles and chats with Gary as we wind our way through the packed restaurant. It's filled with antiques and is surprisingly cozy and warm, despite the chill the hostess has reserved for me. Finally she gestures to my assigned seat. It faces the wall. Gary, however, has a view of the entire restaurant. Before leaving, she gushes, "By the way, Mr. Germain, I loved your show last night!"

He winks and slips her a twenty-dollar bill.

"What show?" A waiter hands us menus.

"*Family Francisco*," Gary boasts. "It's number one in its time slot."

I know the show. It's one of Chessy's favorites.

"Are you the director?"

"Producer. So tell me, what is it you want to say to Gunnar?"

"Do you know him?" I ask, leaning forward.

Gary takes off his sunglasses and studies my face. "It's possible." I begin to squirm. Maybe he has bad news. Is my father dead? In prison? Maybe he doesn't want to meet me. I sit still and wait for Gary to say something, but instead he opens the menu. Then, without looking up, he says, "I'm Gunnar."

I take in a sharp breath. He's my biological father? I'm sitting at a table with my father? I seem to have lost the ability to speak, but my father doesn't seem to notice. Instead, he keeps talking all casual, like he has these kinds of conversations every day. "I changed my name years ago. Gunnar Gerlach was my full name. Gary Germain sounds better, don't you agree?" I nod. No wonder I couldn't find him. "So," he says as he closes the menu. "Here I am. What is that you want?"

"I want to know . . ." I stammer. "I think you may be my father."

He folds his hands. I take note of the gold wedding band. "Did your mother tell you I'm your father?"

I shake my head.

"Have you seen your birth certificate?"

I shake my head again.

"So why do you think I'm your father?"

I take the photo out of my purse and hand it to him. He barely glances at it, then gives it back to me. "Is this is all you have to go on?"

I clear my throat and push forward. "Well, the date is about right, and Chessy, that's my mother, did say that my father was a big shot in Hollywood."

"We'll need tests. How's the fish today?"

I look up to see a waiter standing next to the table.

"It's excellent, Mr. Germain. The swordfish can be prepared Cajun-style, the way you like it."

"Okay, give me the swordfish, and the girl will have the same." He looks at me. "Unless you'd like something else?"

"No, no, that sounds great."

I hate swordfish.

"So," Gary says, as he sips his second unsweetened iced tea, "I'm not saying I am your father, and I'm not saying I'm not your father. It's just that, well, we need to confirm things. I hope you understand." I nod. "And then, say I am your father — then what? What is it you want?"

"I don't know," I begin to falter as I pick apart a piece of bread. "I just wanted to meet you."

"What about your mother?" His eyes narrow. "What is she after?"

"She isn't after anything," I say.

"So let me make sure I have all the facts. You think I'm your father because of one old photo." I nod. "And you just wanted to meet me." I keep nodding. "And your mother didn't put you up to this." I feel like a bobblehead doll.

Our salads arrive, but I'm not hungry. As Gary munches on a tomato, his eyes go back and forth between me and his Blackberry. "Well," he says out of nowhere, "Daniel Jones's documentary was brilliant. You have a strong screen presence, are you aware of that?"

I switch out of bobblehead mode and shake my head no. "You saw the documentary?" I croak.

"I was supposed to meet you there, remember? But you stood me up." For a split second he looks scary. Then Gary puts on a smile. "Anyway, the camera loves you. Like in that one scene where you slowed down so that fat boy wouldn't be last during P.E. That was a tearjerker. He wanted to quit, but you wouldn't let him. You even let him beat you."

Hollywood got that on film?

"Or the scene where that little weird kid, the one who talks a lot, is dumped in the trash can and gets stuck, and you pull him out and give him that pep talk. You come off sounding like a teenage Oprah. Excellent stuff. The film had pacing, pathos, emotion, and at the center of it all was you.

"By the end when you decide to look for me, I was bawling like a baby. You connect with the camera. Do you know how many actors would kill for that?"

Why is he talking about the documentary? The camera? Why isn't he talking about us? The swordfish arrives. Gary doesn't seem to notice that I don't touch my food. He's too busy telling me about me and I'm too stunned to say anything. I'm sitting across from my father. I check to see if there's any resemblance. We do have the same green-grayish eyes. His left ear sticks out a little. So does mine.

I tune in to hear Gary still talking. ". . . that one scene where Daniel does the quick cuts of your different hair colors? Brilliant. The many shades of Maybe. Love it. It's your signature. And then when you're angry about your mother. Compelling. So compelling. By the way, what's with the scarf?" he asks, motioning to my head.

"Why didn't you stay?" I blurt out.

Gary shakes his head like I've snapped him out of a dream. "What? For the film? I saw the whole thing."

"No, in Florida," I say. "With my mother."

For the first time he looks uncomfortable. "We were just having fun. Nothing serious. Besides, Chess always knew I'd be leaving. She told me she had a miscarriage. If she had let me know she was still pregnant, I would have done right by her."

"You would have married her?" For a moment I imagine the three of us — Gary, me, and my mom — sitting in The Ivy having lunch.

He slowly shakes his head. "Noooo, that's not what I said."

"But you said . . ."

Then it dawns on me. I feel so stupid. I look down at my napkin. "Do you have other kids?" I mumble.

Gary signals the waiter for more iced tea. "I don't want to get into personal stuff." He points at my plate. "You haven't touched your lunch. You're not anorexic, are you? So many of the girls are these days. It's not attractive. All these eating disorders — why do girls do that? I don't get it."

I pretend to be interested in my food. He doesn't want to get personal? This man just told me he wished I had been aborted, and he doesn't want to get personal?

"What does your mother think about you trying to find me?"

"She doesn't know I'm doing this. I'm just here on . . . on vacation. I'm staying with my stepdad."

"You're sure she didn't put you up to this?"

My jaw tenses. "I'm sure."

We eat in awkward silence until Gary says, "Maybelline, you need to take a DNA test."

I feel my face burn red, like it's just been slapped. "I just wanted to meet you," I stammer. "And now that I have, we don't ever need to do this again. In fact, we can pretend this never happened."

It's like he hasn't heard a word I've said. Gary takes a small white envelope out of his briefcase. "It's prepaid. Just fill out the form, give them some saliva samples, and we'll be sure. You can even mail it. Simple, right? When you get the results, call me at the office." He hands me his business card.

I shove the test and his card into my purse.

The waiter brings a dessert tray. "Lemon cake?" Gary asks. I shake my head. I can't wait for lunch to be over. As he orders cake and coffee for both of us, I note that his hair is thick and wavy. Mine's more like my mom's.

"Tell me about you and my mother," I ask. My voice sounds flat.

"Honestly, I hardly remember her." He drinks his coffee black. Chessy and I both use lots of cream and Sweet'N Low. "It was a lifetime ago."

"I know. It was *my* lifetime."

"Huh? Oh, right. Well, she really wanted to be a star. That's why she called me. I was a Hollywood talent scout back then. Chess said she was Miss Florida and her talent was exceptional. So I set up an audition and she did her act from the pageant."

"What was her talent?" In all the years of talking about beauty pageants, Chessy's never told me about her talent.

"She had a magic act and claimed she could make things disappear."

"Could she?"

He laughs. "No. It was so obvious she was faking it, but Chess was so damn pretty it distracted from her lack of talent. So we had some fun, and then it was over."

"Just like that?"

"Yeah. Just like that."

"So my mom really wanted to be a star?"

"Sure. Her dream was to conquer Hollywood."

And she ended up running a charm school in Kissimmee, Florida.

"She had big plans," he says.

But instead she had me.

"Why didn't you make her a star? You could have, right?"

Gary takes a sip of coffee, then leans back in his chair. "She wasn't good enough."

"Not good enough?" I ask dryly. "Good enough for what? Good enough for you? She was good enough for you to sleep with!"

"Whoa, whoa, Maybelline, baby. I'm sensing some issues here."

"I'm not your baby."

Gary's eyes narrow and his voice hardens. "I never said you were."

I've heard enough. I rise and push past the beautiful people to get to the door. Gary chases me. "Maybe, stop! Wait up!"

I'm outside but he's still calling my name. I slow down. Maybe he's reconsidered everything. Maybe he's sorry. Maybe he wants to get to know me and be the father I've been looking for. I turn around and face him. The sun glares in my eyes and I can't see straight. Gary is coming toward me with his arms outstretched.

I hesitate. This can't be happening, but it is, it really is. I laugh at how foolish I was. He was probably just testing me. I reach toward him, eager to feel his embrace after all these years. My father pulls me close. I can smell his cologne — some sort of spice. He presses something into my hands and whispers, "Listen, kid. I'm married. My wife and children mean the world to me and I'd never want to hurt them. Stay away, okay? If the DNA test says you're mine, I'll do right by you."

Then he's gone.

## ★ FIFTY-THREE ★

Ted's supposed to be here. Where is he? Where the hell is he? I run down the street, pushing past people, frantically looking around. Finally I spot him offering a candy cigarette to a couple of actress types. "Ted!"

Ted is tiny, but he somehow manages to fold me into his arms and hug me tight until I stop shaking. "Maybe? Maybe, please," he begs. "People are looking at me. I don't need this unwanted attention. It could hurt my career as a mogul."

"This is not about you," I cry. "This is about me! Why can't something be about me for a change?" I snatch the Warhol scarf off my head and blow my nose into it.

"Christ, Maybe. It's always been about you. Why are we even in California?"

I swallow big gulps of air. "Ted," I wail, "it was awful. I think he's my dad, and he's an asshole! My mother's an idiot and my father's an asshole — so where does that leave me?" Ted starts to say something, but I cut him off. "Don't you dare answer that!"

Ted walks me up and down the street until my breathing returns to normal. When I'm done telling him everything, he whistles. "Wow, I can't believe it!"

"I know," I say, nodding.

"Christian Culver couldn't get a table?"

"Ted, did you hear anything I said about my father?"

"Gunnar is Gary, big producer, doesn't trust you, likes blackened fish, said Chessy's a loser. Yeah, I heard. Hey, are you going to take the DNA test? Can I see it? I've always wanted to take a DNA test. I think I have royal blood."

"I don't know."

"You should," he says as he paws through my purse and pulls out the test packet.

"Why?"

"So you'll know for sure."

"What if I really don't want to know? What if I don't care?" I start wailing again.

"Don't be stupid. Of course you care, or else you wouldn't have taken out an ad. You wouldn't have met this guy for lunch. You wouldn't have come to Los Angeles in the first place. Am I right? Tell me I'm right."

Ted's right.

"Hey, can I have this?" he asks, holding up the DNA packet.

"Why? Sure. Whatever," I mumble. I don't care. It's starting to feel good to cry, like scratching an itch. "Ted," I babble, "things aren't happening the way they're supposed to."

"Come here, Maybe." Ted hugs me tight again and doesn't let go until we near the Rolls. That's when I realize I'm still holding the black pouch Gary had put in my hands.

I open it and scream. My scream startles Ted, and he screams. Then I show him what's inside and he screams again, and I scream some more. He rushes me into the Rolls and slowly we dump the contents of the envelope out — and both start screaming.

"Five thousand dollars," Ted announces when he's finally finished counting the bills. "That's a lot of moola."

"It's my hush fund," I say bitterly. "My payola to keep out of his life. He hinted that if I'm his real daughter, there's more where that came from. More, to make sure I keep quiet so I don't ruin it for his 'real' family."

"What are you going to do with it?"

"I don't know." Suddenly I feel tired. I don't know anything anymore.

## ★ FIFTY-FOUR ★

It took me almost seventeen years, and nearly three thousand miles, to find out that the man who's most likely my father is nowhere near the man I always dreamed he'd be. Where does that leave me now?

With nothing left to lose, I look for Hollywood's documentary. Vilma has leaned it against the dresser mirror next to my pile of socks. She has mended the holes. I clutch the teddy bear and turn on the DVD player in the living room. I'm still numb as I watch the film begin. It's just as painful as I remember. But as it moves forward, something begins to change. That girl, that girl who's me — she's not as bad as I thought she was. In one scene, Ms. Hodor, the librarian, says, "I wish we had more kids like Maybe Chestnut here."

The documentary is coming to a close. "What are you going to do?" Ted is asking in the film.

"I'm going to California."

"What's there?"

"That's what I'm going to find out."

"Are you really going to do it?"

"Maybe someday."

Then the film ends on a freeze frame of me looking hopeful.

I pick up the phone and dial.

## ★ FIFTY-FIVE ★

It's almost midnight. I am in my room reading *A Little Princess*. The phone rings. "Sorry for calling so late." It's Hollywood. "But I didn't get your message until after I got back from the movies. Can I come over?"

"Now?"

"Please, Maybe."

It seems like as soon as I hang up the phone, the doorbell rings. Hollywood looks scared.

"I'm sorry I punched you," I tell him. "But you were a jerk for not warning me about the film."

"I thought I did."

"Whatever."

Hollywood gazes at me, then says, "I like your hair."

I run my fingers through what's left of it. "You liar," I say.

Hollywood looks like he's crumbling. He begins to babble, "In *Rebel Without a Cause,* one of the characters plunged off the cliff in his car. Before the film was released, James Dean died in a car crash. Many people think his death wasn't an accident, but that it was suicide." He pauses and his eyes widen. "Life imitating art. Or maybe it would be death imitating art.

"'I don't know what to do anymore. Except maybe die,'" Hollywood says quietly.

"Hollywood?"

"I'm quoting James Dean in *Rebel Without a Cause*."

"Oh."

"Maybe, if you ever think I would purposely hurt you, I would want to die. I *would* want to kill myself."

I roll my eyes. He's starting to sound Ted-ish. "Come on," I say, walking him toward the patio. We both lean against the rail and look at the ocean. There is a warm breeze as the last of the Santa Ana winds brush past us.

"Ted told me about your meeting with your father," Hollywood says.

"What did he tell you?"

"That he's a jerk."

"Yep, that pretty well sums it up."

"What was it like, meeting him after all these years?"

In the moonlight I spot a trio of birds walking on the beach. They run away from the water when the waves lap the shore.
"At first I was thrilled. Then when he ended up being such a bastard, I hated him. Now? Now, I don't know what to think. I mean, it's not for sure that he's my father — but something tells me he is. And you know what? I don't want it to be him."

We're both silent again. Hollywood tugs on his collar. "Maybe, do you still hate me?"

I hesitate. No sense in letting him off easy. After allowing a decent amount of time to pass, I answer, "No, I don't hate you, Hollywood. How could I?"

Even though I am staring straight ahead, I can feel the weight lift off of Hollywood's shoulders as he sighs.

I turn to face him. "Why did you make that documentary?"

Hollywood flinches, then stammers, "It wasn't something I planned. Not in the beginning, at least. I was always filming you because . . . well, because. Then I got the idea to make a documentary. I read that when you do one, the subject should be something dynamic. Something you care about a lot."

Now it's my turn to be silent. Finally I say, "I don't want you filming me anymore."

"Okay," Hollywood says flatly. "But Maybe, did you ever watch the DVD I left for you?"

"You left that, and the teddy bear and chocolates too?" He nods. I take a breath. The salty air gives me the nudge I need before plunging in. "I thought that girl on the screen was really messed up. But whoever made the film believes in her. I thought, *Why the hell did Hollywood do this to me?* and then I realized he didn't do any of this. I did it all to myself. He just happened to be there. He's always there for me, and he's my friend, no matter what."

"Hollywood, are you crying?"

"No!" He won't look at me. "Hey Maybe," Hollywood says. His voice cracks. "Do you think . . . is it possible . . . I mean, do you have any feelings for me at all?"

Hollywood looks straight into my eyes. He's never done this before, not without a camera between us. Hollywood has beautiful eyes. They're blue.

I laugh, not because it's funny, but because I love Hollywood so much. But not that way. "Oh Hollywood, getting involved with me would just mess you up."

"But I'm already involved with you and messed up," he pleads.

"Sorry, but no. What about Jess?"

"Jess is great, but she's not you."

"Lucky Jess! Hey Hollywood?" I get serious. "There is one thing I need to ask you."

"Anything."

"That part in the film when my mom says, 'Maybelline thinks I don't love her, but I do.' Hollywood, did you put her up to that?"

He shakes his head. "She was drinking when she said that, but it doesn't mean it's not true."

"Thanks, Hollywood. That's what I needed to hear." I lean over and kiss him on the cheek. He looks surprised but not unhappy. "Christ, Maybe," he says. "You're such a tease."

I take Hollywood by the hand and lead him into the house. Then I give him a gentle shove out the front door. "Good night, Hollywood."

"If I can't make movies about you, can I at least dedicate them to you?" he asks as he walks backward down the driveway.

"Good night, Hollywood," I say, laughing. "Go home."

After he leaves, there's one more thing I need to do. I take out my father folder. Who was I trying to kid? I guess I always knew that none of these men were my dad. One by one, I tear the pictures into tiny pieces. I stop and stare at the photo of my mother and Gary before ripping it in half.

I head to the patio. Hollywood's left his Super 8 behind. It's lighter than I thought it would be. I turn it on, then toss the bits of paper over the balcony. Through the lens, I watch the Santa Anas sweep them away. When there's nothing left to film, I turn off the camera and go to bed.

## ★ FIFTY-SIX ★

In the morning, I wake up to find Chessy's photo in my hand. The other half is gone. My mother looks so young and happy.

As soon as Willow and Sammy leave, I call a cab. There's someplace I need to go and I don't want to have to ask anyone for a ride. When the taxi shows up, I get in. "Gateway Travel Agency," I tell the driver.

## ★ FIFTY-SEVEN ★

**W**illow's home when I get back. I need another ride, and this time I ask her. She drives like a maniac, but I can't complain since she's doing me a favor. As we careen down the hill, I grip the box that's resting on my lap. It's too big for me to carry to the taco truck.

After she drops me off, Willow waves to Jess, guns the engine, and is gone. Jess lights up when she sees me. "Maybe, I've missed you!"

"It must have been hard having to do all the work yourself."

"No, silly, I've missed you. Talking to you, having fun. It's not about the work, although I must admit things went a lot more smoothly around here when it was the two of us."

"This is for you," I say, handing the box over. It's big and flat. Jess looks at me, questioning. "Just open it," I tell her.

"Oh Maybe!" she whispers as she admires Sammy's photos.

"I like the one of you and me tossing tortillas to each other," I tell her.

"It's my favorite too." Even though it's late in the afternoon and we usually shut down at this time, Jess immediately starts putting the food photos up. The magnets on the backs work as well as I had hoped they would. "Maybe, how can I repay you and Sammy?"

"Jess, this is my way of repaying you!"

"For what?"

"For saving me."

"From what?"

"From Tammy, Todd, and Tina. From boredom. From — I don't know! And Sammy doesn't want anything from either of us. He'd be insulted if we tried to pay him. That's just the way he is."

I jump into the truck and automatically start cleaning the grill. Jess joins me and puts away the big plastic shakers of spices. "You still mad at Danny?" she asks.

"Not anymore."

"Good," she says. "It was tearing me up that the two of you weren't speaking. He's really talented, isn't he?"

I nod. "Yeah, Hollywood's pretty amazing."

"Who's Hollywood?"

"I mean Daniel. Daniel's really something."

"You are too," Jess says. "Seeing you in the documentary made me cry, but a good cry."

We work in silence. Jess and I don't need to pollute the air with small talk. It feels good to be back in the truck. The smells of onions and pickled radishes and jalapeños are better than any fancy perfume.

After the truck is clean, Jess hands me a guava Jarritos and we sit and admire Sammy's food photos.

"Jess, can I ask you something?"

"What?"

"Are you going to go to Princeton?"

"You know about that?"

"I saw the letter."

Jess swirls what's left of her soda around in the bottom of the bottle.

"I'm not going."

"Why not? I thought you wanted to be a lawyer."

"My uncle needs me. . . ."

"But Jess, this is your life we're talking about, not his."

"I know, but . . . I can't explain it. It's like, it's not up to me."

"Does your mom even know you got accepted?"

"I didn't even tell her I applied. I just did it to see if I could make it. I never thought I really would get in." She hesitates. "This may sound weird, but I was so much happier before I knew Princeton wanted me."

Jess looks so sad. I'm kind of sorry I brought it up. I try to change the subject. "Hey Jess, I've been thinking about the truck and I have some ideas."

She looks grateful to be talking about something else. "What?"

"Well, what if we had a list of seven things, you know, like promises to the customer."

"Oh! You mean, like a mission statement? Things like, 'Our ingredients will always be fresh.'"

"Exactly. And how about 'Every taco is made to order . . .'"

We spend the rest of the afternoon talking, and laughing, and coming up with ideas. We name our list "The Benito's Taco Truck Tenets." As I am about to leave, Jess asks, "I'll see you tomorrow, right?"

"See you tomorrow, Jess."

"Hey Maybe, there is one more thing. I like your hair. But would you mind wearing a baseball cap next time? You might scare the customers."

I laugh and head home.

## ★ FIFTY-EIGHT ★

The sound of the traffic and the crash of the waves make an unlikely duet that somehow works. Another new construction site has gone up overnight. This is good news for Benito's Taco Truck #4. Luckily, the photos Sammy took help speed things up. Jess added the name of each taco and a number. Now most people just yell out things like, "Three number twos, hold the onions."

Today is hotter than usual and we're working on hyperspeed. Still, I find the hard work relaxing — and a great way to get my mind off of Gary or Gunnar or whoever he is or isn't.

Jess slaps down a tortilla, I scoop up some carne asada and toss it on, she puts it on a plate, I garnish it and hand it out the window. "Uncle Benny scowled when he first saw the photos," Jess says as she stirs the rice on the back burner. Expertly, she tosses peppers into an iron skillet lined with hot oil. "But when I showed him the day's receipts, he rubbed his head and asked, 'Muchacha, how can you do this all by yourself? Your truck has been bringing in more money than all of the others.' That's when I told him about you."

I look up from the grill. Jess has always been afraid to mention me to her uncle Benny. "What did he say?"

"He said, 'She's not Mexican?' and I said, 'No, but she's my friend.' I explained that the photos were your idea and how I couldn't have done any of this without you. And do you know what he said?"

I shake my head. I'm not sure I want to know. I've had enough rejection to last me a while.

"He said, 'I will not have a *gringa* on my truck!'" I spill the salsa, but quickly wipe it up. Jess lowers her voice to imitate her uncle. "'Our family's reputation is at stake!'

"I told him you were a great cook and he said, 'Then she'll have to prove it to me.' So I told him that you would!"

"What? Jess, I can't do that!"

"Why not? You'll do fine. What do you think you've been doing all summer? Anyway, you don't have a choice. He's coming tomorrow." Jess's eyes are bright and I can tell she's excited about this.

I shake my head slowly. "No, I'm sorry, Jess, but I won't do it."

The chicken on the grill begins to turn brown, but Jess doesn't take her eyes off of me. "Maybe, I need you to do this. I need to prove to Uncle Benny that I can run this truck, I can hire someone, I can make money, and that I'm just as good or better than all the guys who run the other trucks. Please, Maybe."

The chicken is now burning. Jess's eyes stay on me, pleading. Finally I nod. "Sure. Okay. Whatever."

Jess gives me a hug then turns her attention to the burnt chicken. She expertly scrapes it off the grill and throws some water on what's left. A huge flume of steam rises, but Jess doesn't seem to notice as she discards the burnt bits. When she's done, the grill looks brand-new.

"Daniel and I went to the movies last night," Jess says cheerfully. "Maybe, he finally kissed me!"

"That's nice." I don't tell her who he saw after the movies.

"It was nice," she says softly. Even though it's ten thousand degrees in the taco truck, I can see Jess blush. "Have you ever met someone that you just totally click with?"

Well, there's Ted, but I know that's not what she means. "Not yet," I tell her. "When it comes to relationships, I've seen too many bad ones."

On the walk home I begin thinking about the summer ending. No one has mentioned it. Not Ted, not Hollywood, not Jess, not Sammy. It's as if by ignoring it, it won't happen. I contemplate not showing up tomorrow so I won't have to cook for Uncle Benny. God, why did I ever agree to it? It reminds me of my last days as a beauty pageant contestant. I just hated it, but Chessy kept pushing me. She pushed and pushed until one day I threw up onstage. I never had to enter another beauty pageant after that.

But this is different. Though I don't want to compete, I want to win. I want to show Uncle Benny that I am worthy of Benito's Taco Truck #4. I want to keep this job. I need to keep it. I'm not going back to Kissimmee, ever.

What would have been my mother's wedding day is coming up. I wonder if she got the present I sent.

## ★ FIFTY-NINE ★

I get to work early, just as the taco truck pulls up. Jess has posted our list of Benito's Taco Truck Tenets where everyone can see it. When I don't see anyone inside with her, my pace picks up. Hopefully Uncle Benny's a no-show. Just thinking about the test has left my stomach in knots.

"Hey Jess. Is the torture test still on?"

"Yep. Uncle Benny's coming after the lunch rush. Now, Maybe," Jess lowers her voice even though there's no one around. "Do your best. You know, just do what you've been doing all summer. When Uncle Benny does his taste test, he'll see how great you are."

"You did fine on your own before you met me," I protest.

Jess acts like I've thrown a glass of water on her. "*Maldita sea,* Maybelline, what is your problem? You're a wonderful cook, you can do this —"

"No I can't! Jess, I don't want to be in some competition. Besides, why is Uncle Benny getting so bent out of shape? It's just tacos."

"It's not 'just tacos,'" Jess says angrily. "I can't believe you

**238**

would say that." She turns her back to me and takes out the tortillas. "Do whatever's best for you, Maybe. I don't care."

The silence echoes in the taco truck.

"Here, give those to me," I offer, reaching for the tortillas. Jess ignores me. The truck feels like it's getting smaller. I finish slicing the limes and then step out to get some air. Maybe I'll just go to Sammy's. Jess is fine on her own. She really doesn't need me. I would just embarrass her in front of Uncle Benny.

I can hear Jess calling after me as I cross the busy highway. The line outside the truck is starting to form. Jess motions for me to come back, but I don't respond. After a while she gives up.

## ✦ SIXTY ✦

*H*ONK! Someone is honking at me. "Hey, baby, want a lift?"

"Ted, what are you doing here?"

"I'm hungry. Plus I'm picking up a painting for Miss de la Tour and I was in the neighborhood. Why are you standing over here? Shouldn't you be in there?" he says, gesturing to Benito's Taco Truck #4.

There are only a few people milling about the truck now. I check my watch. Was I standing in the same spot for almost three hours? I adjust my baseball cap.

"Jess wants me to cook for Uncle Benny," I try to explain. "He doesn't want a *gringa* on the truck unless she can cook. I guess he's afraid I'm going to be an embarrassment to the taco world."

Ted flips open his cigarette case and takes out two candy cigarettes. He tucks the second one behind his ear. "Well, let's think about this. Yeah, you could be an embarrassment, I can see that."

"Gee, thanks, friend."

"I was going to add that on the other hand you could be a credit to taco eaters everywhere. But now I'm not going to say that. Nor am I going to mention that your running away from everything is getting redundant. Nor am I going to say that Jess saved your sorry butt by giving you a job. Otherwise you'd be wiping up barf from Ike and Tina Turner, or whoever you were supposed to babysit."

Crap. Why does he always do this to me?

"You know what I think?" I ask.

Ted gives me a smug smile. "Actually, I do. Come on." He holds out his arm and I take it.

"Why did the Maybe cross the road?" Ted asks as we dodge the cars.

"To get to the other side," I answer.

Jess is cleaning up. She greets Ted warmly but ignores me. I bend down to pick up some trash. "You don't need to do that," Jess says coolly.

"I want to."

"I thought you didn't work here anymore."

"She's sorry she's screwing everything up," Ted explains as he admires the taco photos. "I'll take a number three and a number seven."

"Maybelline, you're such a pain," Jess says, shaking her head.

"So I've been told. I'm sorry, Jess. Really. I think I'm just nervous."

Jess's smile warms me. "Nothing to be nervous about, Maybe. Just be yourself."

In no time, Jess and I are back in the truck laughing and talking. This feels like home and I'm having so much fun that I'm taken off guard when a maroon Chevy Monte Carlo pulls up. Los Lobos blasts from the car.

"Uncle Benny," Jess whispers.

Quickly, I wipe my hands on a paper towel and follow Jess. Ted has already cornered him. "You're scary Uncle Benny?" he squawks. Both Jess and I groan at the same time. "I thought you'd be really old with a big fat belly. How old are you?"

"I'm twenty-eight," Uncle Benny says. He looks confused as Ted grills him about his work, the silver hood ornament on his car, and his choice of hair-care products.

Uncle Benny wears the scowl of a male model. His black hair is slicked back, but there's a wave to it. His mustache is trimmed neatly, and his muscles bulge beneath his Benito's Taco Truck T-shirt.

". . . so I told Maybe — that's her over there." Ted gestures to me. I give Uncle Benny a small wave. "I told her, why are you scared of Uncle Benny? You haven't even met him yet. And she said, 'What if he's a jerk . . .'"

I hide in the truck. I can't take this.

"Maybe?" It's Jess. "Come on out. I want you to meet him."

As Jess pushes me toward Uncle Benny, Ted is still going full force. Now he's talking about Gloria de la Tour.

"I thought she died a long time ago," Uncle Benny says.

"I know!" Ted says, waving his arms. "That's why I am orchestrating her comeback."

"Uncle Benny," Jess interrupts. "This is my friend Maybe."

I feel myself shrinking as he looks me over. He scowls. "So you think you can make tacos?"

"She has been. All summer. And they're good," Jess says.

"We'll see." Uncle Benny crosses his arms. The skull tattoo on his biceps makes me cringe. "Benito's Taco Trucks have a reputation to uphold. It's a family-run business, and we've never had an outsider work for us before. You're not even Mexican."

Uncle Benny is staring at me so hard that I wonder if he can see me back in Kissimmee living above a charm school. I take a deep breath and raise my eyes to meet his glare. "I can understand why you would want to make sure that you have only the best on your taco trucks. Otherwise, you wouldn't have Jess. But she's the one who trained me, and you'll see that she's good at what she does."

I turn toward the truck, then call out, "What would you like me to make?"

"Everything."

"Everything?"

"Everything."

Slowly I step into the taco truck. It feels like the first time I've ever been here. I tie a fresh apron around my waist and fire up the grill and the burners. At first I overcook the carne asada, so I have to do it over. I sprinkle too many onions on the carnitas. I spill the salsa. But after a while, I start getting into a rhythm and stop thinking about Uncle Benny. Instead I think about tacos.

A good taco is like a work of art. It's not showy or pretentious. It's unfussy. It's familiar, yet each bite is like a wonderful surprise. The meat is grilled just right — slightly crisp on the edges, but juicy and tender when you bite down. We use only fresh ingredients like firm red tomatoes and deep green cilantro. The onions are caramelized or chopped, depending on the order. Handmade yellow corn tortillas are warmed on the grill, never served cold. They are thick enough to hold the taco, but they don't overwhelm the fillings or fall apart.

The salsa is made daily. The guacamole is hand-mashed and chunky, using ripe California avocados, green onions, and spices.

The carrots and radishes that are served on the side are pickled and crunchy. But really, it's all about the taco.

Each taco is made fresh. I can size up a taco eater by the way he orders. Jess has taught me to listen to the customer. If they hesitate or ask questions, they're a newbie and we should go mild on them, even if they ask for hot. "You can ramp up the heat later, but you can't take it down," she once said.

I've seen men come here hungry and in foul moods, and I've watched their faces change when they take their first bite. I've seen them eat eagerly, lick their fingers, and use a bit of tortilla to sop up the juices and scoop up the last bit of meat. I've watched them return to work happy and satisfied, ready for whatever comes their way.

A taco is not just a taco.

For the next hour I am chopping, grilling, seasoning. I even whip up a batch of salsa when we've run out. Jess races back and forth between the truck and Uncle Benny. With each taco I send out, I feel better. I am actually enjoying myself. Anything Uncle Benny asks for, I can make. Plus I'm fast.

"You're doing great," Jess whispers. "He practically smiled a couple of times."

As Jess takes out a plate of al pastor, I yell out, "Tell him to have it with an orange Jarritos to balance the taste."

I make the last taco of the day, then turn off the grill and the burners. This one's for me. Carnitas, chopped onions, cilantro, a squeeze of lime, salsa, and a generous portion of guacamole. Exhausted and exhilarated, I sit across from Uncle Benny and say, "Not bad for a *gringa,* eh?"

He fixes a stern look on his face, then raises his soda bottle to me. "Maybelline, consider yourself Mexican."

Jess and I high-five. Uncle Benny laughs.

"See, I told you!" Ted says, shoving me.

"So, your dad took those?" Uncle Benny asks, motioning to the numbered taco photos up on the truck. He doesn't look as scary anymore.

I nod without bothering to correct him.

"Business has picked up," says Jess. "I've even created combinations for people who don't have a lot of imagination. Have you seen this?" she asks, pointing to Benito's Taco Truck Tenets. "It was Maybe's idea."

"This friend of yours is quite a businesswoman," Uncle Benny says. "Where does she get it from?"

"She gets it from her mother," Ted answers. "But she'll deny it!"

## ✯ SIXTY-ONE ✯

**A**s Ted drives me up the hill to Sammy's, a taxi comes around the corner and almost hits us. "Watch where you're going!" Ted shouts, shaking his fist like an old man.

I'm in too good a mood to berate cab drivers. Uncle Benny likes my tacos! I've got a bag of them for Willow and a couple of jars of salsa for Sammy from Jess. I'm going to suggest that Uncle Benny bottle and sell the salsa in stores.

"I've gotta get this painting to Miss de la Tour," Ted says as he drops me off. "You did great today, Maybe. You're not a total loser, even if you look like one."

I shove Ted and he shoves me back, and we both grin like idiots.

I float into the living room. Willow is sitting ramrod straight on the couch, facing someone whose back is to me. When she sees me, Willow rises and walks slowly in my direction as if she has a plate on her head and an egg on the plate. I think she's going to stop and talk, but instead she hisses through gritted teeth, "Don't you people ever call first?" Then she keeps walking right out the front door.

Slowly, I approach the couch. I can smell the Shalimar perfume.

"Chessy?"

My mother turns around and stands up. She is in all her glory, wearing what looks like a new peach-colored Ridgeway original. Full makeup. Big hair. She takes one look at me and says, "Maybelline, what did you do to yourself this time?"

"Hello Mother," I say, touching what's left of my hair. "Welcome to California."

I am about to say something more when I see her eyes well up with tears. Mine do the same. She takes a tentative step toward me and I meet her halfway.

Our hug is awkward, but I'll take it. Neither of us knows what to do afterward. Finally, I say, "So I assume you got my present."

Chessy dabs her eyes with a tissue. "You know I don't fly economy. But since you sent a first class ticket, I decided I may as well come for a little visit."

"I'm glad you did."

My mother takes a piece of paper out of her purse and slips on her reading glasses. She clears her throat and begins. "Maybelline, I am aware that my past actions may have caused you pain. I know my drinking has been a hardship —"

"What are you doing?"

Chessy glares at me. "Jesus, Mary, and Joseph, Maybelline! Would you let me finish? I have to do this. It's part of AA's twelve-step program, okay? Apologizing to you is number nine."

"Go right ahead," I say.

She adjusts her glasses and starts over. "Maybelline, I am aware that my past actions may have caused you pain. I know my drinking has been a hardship and I pledge to make amends for all the suffering I may have caused you." She puts the paper down. "I'm sorry, Maybelline." When I don't respond immediately, my mother says, "Perhaps you didn't hear me. I said I'm sorry."

My breathing quickens as I flash back to her drinking, to her put-downs. To Jake. I look at my mother sitting on the couch clutching her piece of paper. She doesn't look like the confident beauty queen she once was. She looks like someone who's scared.

"I am too," I say.

Chessy looks relieved. Then, as if the past few minutes never existed, she says, "So, tell me, how's the taco truck business?"

"You know about that?"

"Of course. You don't think I'd let you come all the way to California and not know what you've been up to. What kind of mother do you think I am?"

I don't answer. Damn that Ted. He's been telling her what I've been doing all this time?

"It's good," I stammer. "The tacos are good. And you, how are you?"

"Well, it's a miracle that I made it here in one piece. The stewardesses were so unaccommodating. Every time I asked for something like an extra pillow or more ice to freshen my drink, they'd act like it was uncalled for. And they looked so frumpy. I always thought stewardesses were supposed to be glamorous. They could use some of Chessy's Charm School, let me tell you.

"Oh! And my luggage. My luggage has gone missing, can you believe that? They claimed they will locate it and deliver it this evening. By the way, do you think Sammy would mind if I stayed here?"

My mother got on a plane to see me *and* she said she was sorry. Is this really happening?

Chessy appraises the room. "My, my, my, Mr. Sammy Wing looks like he's done pretty well for himself. Very nice," she murmurs. "Very, very nice. This place must be worth well over a million dollars."

My mother then turns her sights on me and frowns. "The hair really is atrocious, worse than before, if you can believe that. You've got some color on your face, that's good, and you look so much better without that Goth girl makeup. However, some mascara and shadow won't kill you. You know, I really do hurt when I see people who could do a better job with their makeup. I'm like the Mother Theresa of makeovers. Maybelline, did you lose weight? It looks like you lost a ton of weight. But your clothes are hideous. . . ."

As she rambles on about what a disappointment I am, I can't help but feel good.

## ★ SIXTY-TWO ★

I t's nighttime. My mother is still here. "What do you mean there's no liquor?" she sounds shocked.

"Chessy, you're not supposed to drink."

"I didn't say I wanted a drink, I just asked if there was liquor in the house. You know, in case of an emergency or something."

"You know that Sammy doesn't drink."

"I would have thought he'd have grown up by now. What about the girl — his girlfriend or whatever — does she drink?"

"Nope. Sammy won't let her."

"That's ridiculous! Besides, she looked like she could use a drink. Did you see how strange she was acting?"

Willow hasn't returned and the airline still hasn't located my mother's luggage. We're both at the dining-room table. "These aren't as good as when they're fresh from the grill," I say as I watch her eat a taco with a fork and knife. "I made them this afternoon."

My mother looks up, surprised. "Maybelline, this is delicious. There's no way you could have made this. You must have had help from Jennifer."

"Her name's Jessica, and no, she didn't help me. I made them by myself. Her uncle Benny came to judge my cooking."

Chessy's eyes flicker with interest. "Did you win?"

"I think so."

"You think so, or you know so? Did you get a trophy?"

I shake my head.

"A crown?" she says.

"They don't give crowns for making tacos," I start to explain. When I see that she's smiling, I smile too. I didn't know Chessy was capable of joking about the beauty pageant business.

"Well, they should give you a crown," Chessy says, taking another bite. "Perhaps cooking tacos is your talent."

I feel warm inside. It makes me feel good to see her enjoying my cooking. When she's on her second taco, I tell her, "I met Gunnar."

Chessy gags, then coughs. She takes a sip of water. "Who?" she asks innocently.

"Gunnar, from Alligator Alley. Only now he goes by the name Gary Germain. Is he my father?"

My mother abandons her tacos and walks around the room, stopping to stare at the ocean. "What does it matter anyway?"

She looks tired. Her makeup is starting to wear thin and I can see the bags under her eyes.

"It doesn't," I tell her. "It doesn't matter. He's a jerk."

Chessy softens. "Do you think so?"

"I really think so."

"He is a jerk," she agrees. She raises her chin and adds, "Of course, Gunnar begged me to marry him. He wanted to bring me to Hollywood and make me a star, you know."

"I know."

"Maybelline," Chessy says my name slowly, drawing it out like a plea. Suddenly she doesn't look so sure of herself. "About Jake . . ."

I shake my head. "Forget it."

My mother's voice wobbles. "I should have . . . I thought . . . I'm sorry."

She says it so softly that I'm not even sure if I heard her correctly. I don't dare ask her to repeat it, though. "Okay," I say. "You're here now. We don't need to talk about it."

Chessy looks relieved. As I clear the table, she explores the house. After opening every closet and drawer, my mother comes back looking flushed. "This house is gorgeous. Why did I ever divorce Sammy?" she asks, not expecting an answer.

She's almost giddy, like we never had our talk. But I'll never forget it.

"I hope he doesn't mind that I'm staying here. That tree person he's dating seemed high-strung. How long has he been seeing her?"

"Her name's Willow, and they've been together for about two years."

"She doesn't know how to use blush," Chessy informs me. She flips open a compact and powders her nose. "She bites her nails, and her hair could be a lot shinier. But she does have excellent posture."

On cue the door opens and Willow walks in. She stops cold and her eyes get big when she sees my mother is still here. Sammy pushes past Willow, almost knocking her over. "Chessy! Why didn't you tell me you were coming?"

They fall into each other's arms.

Willow looks like she is about to crumble. I rush to her side. "It's okay," I assure her.

She's still frozen, except for the tears that are splattering on the floor. "No, it's not," Willow whispers back.

As Sammy leads Chessy to the couch, he seems enthralled as she recounts her totally boring story about lost luggage. He nods with sympathy and laughs at the appropriate moments. It is fascinating to watch the hold my mother has over him. I've seen this a million times with men, yet there is still something mesmerizing and sickening about it.

"So you don't mind me staying here?" Chessy is in full flirt mode, pouring on her southern drawl, batting her eyelashes, and straightening Sammy's collar.

"Of course!" Sammy insists. "Of course, you know that."

Willow flees to the kitchen and I follow to make sure she doesn't do anything stupid. "How long will she be here?" Willow asks as she puts a cigarette to her lips and begins flicking her lighter. She's shaking too much to get a light. I take the lighter from her and throw it in the trash can.

"I don't know."

"Why is she here?"

I think about explaining that I knew she had dumped her fiancé/rapist and that her business was failing. That I knew she was in AA. And that I sent my mother a first-class airline ticket and I included a note that read, "I dare you to come to California," but then I changed it to read, "Please come."

Willow looks pained and is holding her stomach. "Chessy's just on a little vacation," I tell her.

"Well, I hope it's really short. I don't want to lose Sammy."

How can I tell her that I don't want to lose Sammy either — or my mom?

## ★ SIXTY-THREE ★

**M**y mother has taken over. Her luggage has vanished, so she's been doing a lot of shopping. This must be some relief to Willow since Chessy had been wearing her clothes, reinterpreted glamour-queen style, of course. Like taking Willow's favorite blouses and adding shoulder pads to them.

Chessy has maxed out two credit cards, but still she has shown no signs of slowing down. The bathroom has turned into a drugstore with her creams and lotions and makeup and whatnots crowding the counter. We are sharing my room. Her things are everywhere — piles of clothes, shoes on the floor, jewelry on the dresser.

"What's this?" my mother asks, pulling out the giant portrait of herself from the back of my closet.

"That's you."

She studies it. "Sammy should have never taken that."

"I'm glad he did. You look really pretty there without makeup."

"You're wrong," Chessy says. But she doesn't put the photo back in the closet. "You know, I never thought I'd say this, Maybelline, but I preferred your Kool-Aid colored spiky mess of hair over this moth-eaten look. Are you trying to start a trend or something? Because if you are, it isn't working."

Willow is terrified of Chessy and clams up whenever she is around, even though my mother has no problem talking to her.

"Stand up straighter, dear, you're slouching."

"You need a manicure. Have you ever considered using Pearly Pink? It's a beautiful color and it will look better on your skin tone, which is looking a bit washed out, don't you think?"

"A tank top and jeans. That's what you're wearing to the movies? Interesting."

A few words from Chessy will send Willow fleeing.

"What?" my mother says to me. "What did I say?"

I can't help but laugh. She's giving Willow the advice her charm-school students used to pay for. She does that for me too. I can see that now.

I'm not surprised to find Willow hovering in the kitchen gripping a huge hunk of cheese. "She hates me, doesn't she?"

"That's just Chessy's way. She actually thinks she's doing a public service when she tells people what they should do."

Willow has tears in her eyes. This has been happening a lot.

"Aw, come on," I say as I slowly pry her fingers off the cheese. "You have great fashion sense, you don't have to listen to her."

"It's not that." She takes a gulp of air. "Sammy's phone doesn't ring at night anymore." When I don't react, Willow spells it out for me. "It was Chessy he was talking to all those times."

I shut my eyes. Of course! It wasn't Ted who told her what I was up to — it was Sammy. All this time it's been Sammy. Chessy never had to call me when she could get a full report from him. She was spying on me . . . Oh God. She was spying on me just like I was spying on her with Ridgeway.

My silence is scaring Willow. She looks so fragile that I need to say something fast. But the thing I want to say the most, I can't. It would kill her to hear that Chessy wants to marry Sammy again — even if he doesn't even know this yet. "Hey," I say to Willow. "Are you going to take me shopping for something to wear tomorrow night? It's going to be a great party and I really need something nice to distract from my hair."

A hint of a smile appears on Willow's worried face. "Okay, I can do that," she says.

I walk over to her and open my arms. Willow surprises me. For a skinny girl, she has a fierce hug.

## SIXTY-FOUR

**M**y mother and I are in the bathroom, staring at ourselves in the mirror. Everything we need is on the counter.

"Are you sure you want to do this?" Chessy asks.

I take a deep breath. "I'm sure."

"Okay, then," my mother says. "We'll do it your way."

## SIXTY-FIVE

**S**ammy, may I have a minute with you?"

He looks up from his desk. "You shaved your head. What will your mother say about that?"

"She's the one who did it."

Sammy chuckles. "I'll never understand the two of you."

I step forward and hand him a box.

"What is it?"

"Open it." As he unwraps it, the smile on his face grows. "It's a lens," I tell him, even though it's obvious. "For your telescope."

Sammy is speechless. "Maybe," he finally says, his voice cracking. "This looks expensive. You didn't have to do this."

"I wanted to do it. It made me happy to be able to. I used my Benito's money." I take a deep breath. "Um, did Chessy talk to you about her . . . plans?"

Sammy pretends to be studying the lens for the longest time. "Maybelline, I said no. It's not that I don't love her. Or you. It's just that, well . . ."

I let out a sad laugh. "She has a lot of baggage?"

"You could say that."

"She's been in AA and serious about sobering up. We can get her to stay on the wagon and —"

"Maybe," he says gently. "I'm sorry. Things are complicated."

"That's okay," I tell him. "You don't have to explain anything to me."

**M**y mother is adding another layer of mascara to her false eyelashes as I tie my Andy Warhol scarf around my head.

"Sammy told me he said no."

"That's what he said," she says cheerfully. "Hand me my blush, will you?"

"You're okay with that?"

"For now. He's got that Willow girl, not that she's any competition. I give them six months, tops. Then we'll see."

At eleven P.M. Hollywood arrives, wearing his sports jacket. He's cut his hair. It must be an epidemic.

"Did you return the book?" I ask. "How much do I owe?"

"It was weird." Hollywood scratches his chin. "They say no one's checked out *A Little Princess* for over two years. So they were surprised when I returned it."

"Hollywood," Chessy gushes. "You look so handsome, I don't even recognize you!"

Hollywood is on his best behavior around my mother. He opens the door for her, and he has even cleaned the Green Hornet. "James Dean," she says as she slips into the front seat. "I love James Dean. All those old movie stars just oozed glamour, but not these new ones. They don't care how they look in public."

By the time we get to Beverly Hills, Hollywood and my mother have covered the Golden Age of Film. The Green Hornet turns into a driveway. "We're here to pick up Ted Schneider," Hollywood says.

The guard grins, revealing a gold tooth. "So you're Teddy's pals. He's told us all about you guys." He looks at Chessy and puts his hands over his heart. "Gorgeous!"

Chessy smiles demurely and says, "Thank you."

"Hit the gas," I tell Hollywood. "Or that man will be my next stepfather."

Hollywood maneuvers up the long tree-lined drive and parks in front of a huge white mansion with Greek columns. This is where Ted has been hanging out?

The heavy wrought-iron door swings open and Ted pops out. The marble lions flanking the front door look like they could devour him in two bites. "I'm leaving now," he shouts into the house. "I'll give you a full report when I get back. Are you sure you don't want to go?"

We can't hear the reply.

"Miss de la Tour," he says by way of explanation as he climbs in the backseat with me.

"I've read about mansions like these," Chessy says reverently, "but I've never actually seen one this close up."

"If you think this looks good, you should see the inside," Ted tells her. "Plus there's a pool and tennis court in the backyard. Of course, Miss de la Tour never uses them on account of her bad hip, but she keeps them in immaculate condition."

During the entire ride to the Griffith Park Observatory, all Ted and Chessy talk about is the glorious Gloria de la Tour. Hollywood speaks up now and then, adding tidbits of de la Tour trivia. I keep quiet. I have a lot on my mind.

## ★ SIXTY-SEVEN ★

The parking lot is practically empty. It's almost midnight. This was Hollywood's idea. The Griffith Park Observatory is closed. The huge domes that house the telescopes are shut, but the building is illuminated by a warm yellow glow from within. I feel like I'm on a movie set.

Sammy and Willow are waiting by Sammy's telescope. It looks small compared to the observatory. The taco truck is here, and Jess and Vilma are feeding the security guards. Hollywood offers me his arm, but Chessy takes it. "Why, thank you," she coos. "What a gentleman! Maybelline, why don't you make this nice young man your boyfriend?"

"Yeah, Maybelline," Hollywood says, treating me to that crooked smile of his, "why don't you?"

I just laugh.

As we make our way toward the group, Hollywood stops at a bust of James Dean. We pause for a moment of silence, then continue on.

Jess is setting out a feast: carnitas tacos, taquitos, sopitas, burritos, quesadillas. There's also a pile of birthday presents and going-away gifts. You'd think that if you felt both happy and sad, the emotions would cancel each other out. But I feel anything but neutral.

"Sit down, everyone!" Jess calls out. She's flushed from rushing around. "Don't let the food get cold."

Chessy whispers to me, "Is that your taco truck friend?" I nod. "You there, Jennifer! Please come here."

"Jessica, this is my mom, Chessy," I say.

"Hi Chessy." She extends her hand. "Nice to meet you."

Instead of taking her hand, Chessy touches Jess's face and turns it from side to side. "What beautiful bone structure. Are you wearing any makeup?" Jess shakes her head. "Gorgeous, just gorgeous," my mother murmurs while taking her seat. "A natural beauty, imagine that."

The rest of us sit down around card tables. Tonight, Jess has covered them with red paper tablecloths. I am sitting between Chessy and Ted. Sammy rises. "I would like to make a toast to our birthday girl."

Everyone raises their drinks and cheers. I am still blushing as I stand. "I would like to make a toast." My voice shakes. "To my best friend in the entire world. I don't know how I am going to get along without you." I turn to Ted. "I love you and will miss you."

Ted bursts out crying, and then I start crying, and soon everyone joins in — even one of the security guards who stopped by to get more salsa. Ted and I walk over to the railing and look out over the city while the others are eating and talking.

"Why do you have to leave?" I ask. I can see the Hollywood sign. "Chessy says we're getting our own place. You can live with us."

"I miss my mom and dad." Ted bursts out crying all over again. "I'm homesick, okay? Your mom's here, but mine's in Kissimmee. Besides, I have important news for my parents, and I have to tell them in person. I got my lab tests back."

"Ted, are you okay? You're not sick, are you?"

He dabs his eyes with a handkerchief. "I took the DNA test."

"What DNA test?"

"Yours, Maybe. The one you never took. The one that Gary Germie gave to you."

"Why would you do that?"

"Well, it was prepaid, and I'm not one to let something like that go to waste."

"And?"

"And the results on Maybelline Chestnut are that you are a male, and your race is Chinese and French."

"Say that again?"

"You heard me. I'm part Chinese, part French, no part Thai."

"No way!"

"Years and years of Thai upbringing. I've been studying the wrong Asian culture."

"What does that mean?"

"I don't know," Ted muses. "But Maah and Paww are going to go into shock, especially since they've planned a family trip to Thailand for next year."

"And then you'll come back?"

Ted gets unusually quiet. "I need to be with my mother and father for a while. You know how they feel about me."

I nod.

"When will you and Chessy move back to Kissimmee?" Ted asks.

"I don't think I'm ever going back."

"What about your mom?"

"Are you kidding me? She keeps asking Sammy and me why we didn't make her move sooner. It's like she has amnesia and can't remember that the idea of flying and moving out of Florida used to paralyze her with fear. Now, she's totally into the L.A. lifestyle. I've even bought her the Oasis Gardens AA spa package with the money Gunnar gave me. It's a week at the luxury resort and pedicures, facials, and Alcoholics Anonymous meetings are included."

"Sounds totally Chessy to me," Ted muses.

"Hey, there's something I want you to have." I take the Warhol scarf off my head and hand it to Ted.

"You're bald," he announces.

"You're short," I retort.

"Maybelline, Ted," Chessy shouts. "Come over here. I have a surprise for you!"

There are two cakes on the table. One says, BON VOYAGE, TED! and the other reads, HAPPY BIRTHDAY, MAYBE. The letters look like the Hollywood sign.

"Do you like yours?" Chessy asks. "I had it custom-made."

I do like my cake. I love my cake. I nod and give my mother a hug. She looks shocked at first, then hugs me back.

"Well, don't eat too much. Even though you've finally gotten around to losing your baby fat, it can come back on in a second."

"Yessss, Mother."

"How come Maybe gets candles and not me?" Ted complains.

"Here, you big whiner, take half. What's mine is yours."

We blow out our candles and pass out slices of cake. Chessy takes two pieces, one from each of us. As we are laughing and eating cake and making jokes about my hair, or lack of it, silence suddenly sweeps over the group as a Rolls-Royce pulls up. An immaculately dressed chauffeur opens the back door, then stands at attention.

"Don't just stare," Gloria de la Tour bellows. "Someone get me a taco!"

Jess and I both rise at the same time. "I got it, Maybe," she says as she heads to the truck. Ted rushes over to Miss de la Tour and Chessy comes in a close second. Who knew my mother could run so fast in heels? Hollywood and Sammy each reach for their cameras.

Miss de la Tour is petite, practically Ted-sized, but seems larger than any of us. Even though she is old, she is very well preserved. I can understand why Ted claims "Gloria de la Tour is the most beautiful movie star of all time." She wears a poufy mint green dress that makes her look like a fancy dessert with about twelve pounds of pearls around her neck. Her silver hair looks like it could deflect missiles.

"Miss de la Tour," Chessy says, curtsying. "This is an honor. I am a huge fan of yours."

Gloria de la Tour ignores her and turns to Ted. In her distinct clipped voice she asks, "How could you do this to me?"

"What?"

"How could you leave me?"

"I told you," Ted says patiently. "I want to go home and be with my mom and dad."

"You were abandoned, or have you forgotten?"

"That was when I was a baby. My parents adopted me and raised me," Ted corrects her as he adjusts the clasp on her necklace.

"Nonsense! If that's what you want, I will adopt you."

"I've already been adopted."

"My lawyers can fix that."

Jess sets a plate of tacos down at the table. Chauffeur slides a chair out for Miss de la Tour. She sits and takes a bite, then waves her hand in the air. Her diamond rings are the size of marbles.

"Teddy, tell the chef that this is good."

Ted turns to Jess. "This is good."

Jess beams.

"You can't leave, Teddy," Miss de la Tour says, her voice softening. "What will I do without you?"

"We're all going to miss him," I say.

Miss de la Tour notices me for the first time. She looks me up and down. "What's the matter with your hair? Do you have cancer?"

"That's Maybe, my best friend," Ted whispers.

"Ah, I've heard a lot about you. So, you don't want Teddy to leave either then, do you?" I shake my head. "See, Teddy, L'Oréal says to stay too."

"Excuse me, but my name is Maybelline, and I don't want him to go. But if he needs to and wants to, then I think he should."

"Rude girl," Miss de la Tour snaps. "Who asked you?"

I back away, but Ted handles her with ease. "Miss de la Tour, you know how much I love you."

Her eyes get moist as she takes his hands in hers. "I do know that, Teddy. That's why you can't leave me."

"You'll find someone to replace me. Plus you have your staff to look after you."

"If you are referring to Cook, the housekeeper, my lawyer, and Chauffeur, then you know they are just after my money. They all want a spot in my will."

Chauffeur rolls his eyes. Vilma smiles coyly at him and hands him an extra-large piece of cake.

Ted's face is as somber as Miss de la Tour's. Suddenly he lights up. "I know who my replacement is — at least until I get back in a year or two!"

"And whom might that be?" Gloria de la Tour sniffs.

"She's right here."

Ted looks at me and I freak. Uh, no. No, no, no, no. This is just wrong. He comes close, winks, and keeps walking right past me. Chessy looks shocked when Ted takes her hand and pulls her toward Miss de la Tour.

"Ted," my mother hisses. "What are you doing?"

"This is Chessy Chestnut," Ted tells Miss de la Tour, "the woman I have been telling you about. The one who runs the charm school in Florida."

My mother curtseys again. "Miss de la Tour," she says reverently.

"So you think you have what it takes to be my personal assistant, do you?"

Chessy is speechless. Ted speaks up. "She does."

I can tell by the stunned look on my mother's face that this is news to her. Her eyes keep darting to mine. I've never seen her look so unsure of herself.

"Tell me, Miss Chestnut," Miss de la Tour says disdainfully, "who will run the charm school?"

"The charm school has run its course," Ted says. "Chessy is closing it down and moving on."

"So you want to work for me, is that it?"

"She does." Ted nods.

"Why would you do that?"

"Because," Ted tells her, "Chessy feels that it is time for a new chapter in her life. She wants to be here in California with her beloved daughter. And she is just now realizing that she can be of service to you, and at the same time immerse herself in the glamour of Hollywood that is so sorely lacking in Kissimmee, Florida. Isn't that right, Chessy?"

My mother doesn't move. It's like her entire body has been Botoxed.

"That means yes," Ted translates.

Miss de la Tour looks my mother up and down. For once I am glad that Chessy has overdressed. She is wearing an Oscar de la Renta-inspired Ridgeway magenta gown and gold high heels with a small crown tucked into her big hair.

"Teddy's recommendations go a long way with me," Miss de la Tour says. "We will have a trial period of two weeks. During that time, you will live with me in the main house. If you don't work out, Teddy will be obliged to return to Beverly Hills. Do you understand?"

"What about Maybelline?" my mother asks, finally finding her voice.

"What about her?"

"She would need to live with me. She's still in school."

"I'm going to work on the taco truck," I say. "I don't need to go to school —"

"Yes you do," my mother and Sammy say at the same time.

270

"Fine," Miss de la Tour says grudgingly.

"Oh," and Chessy adds. "I can't start immediately. I'm booked at the Oasis Gardens for a week."

"The AA package?" Miss de la Tour asks, looking at my mother with mild interest. Chessy nods. "Excellent choice," Miss de la Tour tells her. "I go myself a couple times a year. All the movie stars do."

My mother glows when she hears this.

Miss de la Tour glances my way. "If she's going to be living in my house, she's going to need some work. She's sort of shabby, don't you think? Hard to believe that she's your daughter. She looks like trouble, and from what I've heard from Ted, she is."

I look at Ted. He shrugs sheepishly. Before I can protest, Chessy speaks up. "Maybelline may look like a slob and a slacker, but that's her choice. Besides, I can't do a thing about her hair until it grows in. Then I'm thinking blonde."

"Or auburn," Miss de la Tour muses.

"Yes, and I'm going to get her into a dress —"

"She'd look good with more color —"

"A nice floral pattern."

"What about makeup?"

"Absolutely."

"A wig!" Gloria de la Tour cries.

"Yes!" Chessy agrees. "You're brilliant!"

As they bond over how pathetic I am, I grab Ted and drag him away again. "You'd think someone would ask me what I want," I tell him.

"What do you want, Maybe?"

*What do I want*, I wonder.

"I want to be somebody," I finally say.

"You already are."

Ted and I are quiet as we watch Hollywood film my mother and the movie star.

"Looks like Hollywood's found his next documentary," I say.

"Do you like him at all?" asks Ted.

"As a friend. As a really good friend."

"But do you think he's gay? You know, the James Dean thing, and he's never gone out on a date, unless you count Jess. But I know for a fact that they haven't really made out, and —"

It suddenly hits me.

"Oh my God," I gasp. "Duh. I get it now. *You* like Hollywood, don't you?"

Ted won't look at me.

"Oh, Ted," I say, reaching to give him a hug.

He punches me hard. "So? So what?" he says defensively.

"You goof," I laugh. "You're right — so what? If Hollywood's who you like, you've got great taste. And so what if you're gay, straight, bi, or tri. I don't care if you're Thai, Chinese, French, or from Mars. You'll still be mine, all mine, no matter what. God, I love you, Thammasat Tantipinichwong Schneider!"

Ted looks relieved. "Don't tell Hollywood, okay?"

"Okay."

"And take good care of Miss de la Tour. She's actually very fragile, despite what she says."

"I will."

"And cross your heart and hope to die and promise, promise me, you'll be good to my best friend Maybelline Mary Katherine Mary Ann Chestnut." His voice cracks. "She really needs a lot of help. In fact, she's pretty hopeless."

By now I'm crying. My heart is breaking into a thousand

pieces. Ted presses something into my hands. It's a cell phone. "So we can keep in touch," he says. "I've programmed my number in. It's speed dial number one and I'm listed as 'National Treasure.'"

Suddenly there's a big gasp from the group. Willow points to the sky and screams, "Look! A wishing star."

I close my eyes and make a wish.

Ted breaks the silence. "You idiots, it's an airplane!"

Sammy looks up from his telescope. "The boy's right," he says.

"Of course I'm right," Ted says. "I always am."

I just laugh. He is so annoying.

"I need more cake," Ted announces.

"You go ahead," I tell him. "I need a minute alone."

## SIXTY-EIGHT

Los Angeles — my new home. The lights shine for miles and wink at me as another plane arches across the sky. Or is it a shooting star? I take my chances and make another wish.

When I look toward the group, no one else seems to have noticed it. Chauffeur is eyeing the leftover tacos as Vilma eyes him. My mother is busy staring at Gloria de la Tour, who is looking at Ted. Ted is gazing at Hollywood as he talks to Jess. Sammy is staring at Chessy, and Willow is watching him. Hollywood glances at me and grins.

"Hey Maybe," Ted hollers. "Get over here! You don't want to miss your own party, do you?"

"Ted's right," my mother calls out. "Maybelline, come back."

I start walking, then pick up speed as I run toward the party. "All right," I shout. "Here I come!"

## ✷ ABOUT THE AUTHOR ✷

When she was little, Lisa Yee could see the Hollywood sign and the Griffith Park Observatory from her house. She attended the University of Southern California (go Trojans!), then spent seventeen years in Florida before returning to the Los Angeles area. She now lives with her family in South Pasadena.

Lisa is the author of *Millicent Min, Girl Genius*, the winner of the Sid Fleischman Humor Award; *Stanford Wong Flunks Big-Time*, an ALA Notable Book for Older Readers; and *So Totally Emily Ebers*. As part of her research for *Absolutely Maybe*, Lisa ate at approximately twenty-four different taco trucks. She recommends the carnitas.

Please visit Lisa's website at http://www.lisayee.com and her LiveJournal at http://lisayee.livejournal.com.

# ALSO FROM
# ARTHUR A. LEVINE BOOKS

By David LaRochelle

By Shaun Tan

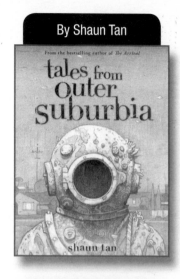

By Francisco X. Stork

By Jaclyn Moriarty

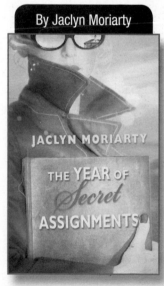

ARTHUR A. LEVINE BOOKS

📖 SCHOLASTIC

SCHOLASTIC and associated logos
are trademarks and/or registered
trademarks of Scholastic Inc.

www.scholastic.com

AALBKSA